A Love to Share

New Hope Falls: Book #9.5

By

KIMBERLY RAE
JORDAN

THREE**STRAND**
P R E S S

A CORD OF THREE STRANDS IS NOT EASILY BROKEN.

A man, a woman & their God.
Three Strand Press publishes Christian Romance stories
that intertwine love, faith and family. Always clean.
Always heartwarming. Always uplifting.

A LOVE TO SHARE/ Kimberly Rae Jordan. -- 1st ed.
ISBN-13: 978-1-988409-71-9

My brethren, count it all joy when you fall into various trials,
knowing that the testing of your faith produces patience.
But let patience have its perfect work,
that you may be perfect and complete, lacking nothing.
If any of you lacks wisdom, let him ask of God,
who gives to all liberally and without reproach,
and it will be given to him.

James 1: 2 – 5 (NKJV)

CHAPTER ONE

Jacob McNamara stared at the tall cop who stood just inside the door to the apartment with Lynn, his best friend's mom. Tucking his shaking hands under his thighs, he gripped the edge of the couch as he glanced over at his best friend. Bobby shrugged before looking back at his mom and the cop.

Bobby might not know what this was about, but Jacob had a pretty good idea. Or maybe it was a bad idea. All he knew was that it wouldn't be anything he wanted to hear.

Lynn turned and walked toward them, gripping some papers in her hands. Her eyes were wide, and her lips were pinched thin, as if trying to hold back her emotions. The cop followed behind her, a serious expression on his face.

Jacob's stomach lurched as the cop, a big burly man, sat down on the ottoman in front of him.

The man gave him a brief smile. "Hi, Jacob. My name is Dan. How're you doing?"

Jacob couldn't handle the small talk. Not when his life was on the verge of changing forever. "She's dead, isn't she?"

Dan let out a sigh, his look sympathetic. "Yes. I'm sorry."

"She killed herself."

The man paused, his brow furrowing. "Why do you say that?"

"She's tried it before." And the signs had been there before he'd left her the previous afternoon. She'd hugged him tighter and longer than usual. Her emotions—which were always near the surface—had overflowed with tears and words. And she'd told him more than once that she loved him fiercely.

But even though the thought of what she might have been planning had been in the back of his mind, Jacob hadn't tried to stay with her. Hadn't done anything to try to stop her. How could he have when he, more than anyone else, had known how desperately depressed and sad she was? But even though he'd known that suicide was likely what would eventually take her from him, he hadn't realized how unprepared he was for the loss.

She had tried to be a good mom. But for as long as he could remember, there had been frequent extended periods of time when she hadn't been able to work. Money had been scarce, and food scarcer. She'd always apologize, crying as she clung to him, for not being able to give him a better life.

It had only been because of the help of sympathetic people, like Lynn, that he hadn't been taken from his mom. As hard as it had been living with her, he hadn't wanted to be separated from her. Because, for everything that she hadn't been able to provide, Jacob had never doubted that his mom loved him, and she'd never done anything to hurt him.

As the realization that he'd never see her again—never feel her arms around him again—sank in, Jacob struggled to breathe, and tears stung his eyes. How was he supposed to live without her? His heart hurt so badly that he looked down at his chest, certain he'd see blood staining his T-shirt.

Even as he tried to grasp the horrible loss he'd just suffered, Jacob hoped his mom was happy wherever she was. He'd miss her terribly, though, and anxiety filled him as he thought about where he'd go now that she wasn't there to take care of him.

Swallowing hard in order to loosen the tightness in his vocal cords, Jacob said, "What's going to happen to me?"

Maybe Lynn would let him stay with them. Or maybe the father he'd never met would finally be willing to take him in.

"Mrs. Devon has agreed to let you stay here with her while we contact your father and make arrangements for you to go to him."

"You know his name?" His mom had rarely spoken about him, just saying that they'd broken up before she'd realized she was pregnant with Jacob. She had never told Jacob what his dad's first name was, though he knew the man's last name, since he shared it with the mystery man.

"Yes. Elijah McNamara."

The name meant nothing to him, but he tried to imagine the type of man who it would belong to. "What if he doesn't want me?"

The cop's smile was kind. "We'll cross that bridge when we get to it, okay? In the meantime, we'll see what he has to say."

Jacob nodded, pulling his hands from under his thighs and wrapping his arms around himself. He was shaking inside, and it felt like he was going to splinter apart, letting all the sadness that had built up inside him gush out.

The enormity of the situation hit him like a sledgehammer. He was all alone in the world.

There might be a man out there who was biologically his father, but that didn't mean he would want Jacob. And if he didn't... there was no one else to take him. To care about him. To love him. He knew his mom had a family, but they hadn't cared about her, so why would they care about him?

Bending his head, Jacob tried to swallow the sob that wanted to erupt from deep inside him. Why hadn't he stopped her? Why hadn't he insisted that he stay with her when she said she'd made arrangements for him to spend the night with Bobby?

A hand landed on his shoulder, squeezing lightly. "It's going to be okay, son."

That was easy for the man to say. His world hadn't just imploded with the death of the only person who had loved him unconditionally.

CHAPTER TWO

Eli McNamara hovered beside the crib, holding his breath as he gazed down at the baby. He seemed to be sleeping, but the little guy had been known to appear asleep, only to begin crying the minute they stepped out of the room.

Holding his breath, he began to slowly move toward the door. Once there, he stepped into the hallway, pulling the door almost all the way shut. He didn't close it, though, as the snick of the knob engaging would probably wake little Noah.

He lingered outside the door for a couple more minutes. Then, when it seemed that the baby was actually going to stay asleep, Eli turned and made his way downstairs.

Noah had been sleeping more fitfully than usual the last few days. Now six months old, he had finally outgrown the colic that had plagued him for the first four months of life. Unfortunately, he still wasn't a great sleeper and had far too many moments where nothing would settle him. He also hated naps, usually waking within half an hour of being put down.

It was a strain for them, but most especially for Anna.

Back in the living room, he peered over the back of the couch to see that Anna was down for a nap as well, so he picked up the baby monitor and went to his workshop. After he set the monitor on his worktable, he sat down with a piece of wood that he'd been working on for a special order. It was a Christmas gift for someone from the church, so he wanted to make sure he had it finished in time.

He'd barely started to work on it when his phone rang. Grateful that whoever it was hadn't called five minutes earlier, Eli pulled his phone out and stared at the display. He didn't recognize the number and almost didn't pick up the call, but something prompted him to tap the screen to accept it.

"Hello?"

"May I speak with Elijah McNamara?" a woman asked, her words holding a bit of an accent that he couldn't place.

"Speaking."

"Do you know a Sheila Thompson?"

The name caught Eli so off-guard that, for a moment, he didn't respond.

"Hello? Mr. McNamara?"

"Yes. I'm here. Sorry. It's just been awhile since I've heard the name. Why are you asking about Sheila?"

"I regret to inform you that Miss Thompson has passed away."

Eli slumped against the table. "What?"

"Miss Thompson took her life two days ago," the woman said, setting off a wave of grief and disbelief inside Eli. Sheila had committed suicide? "And she left instructions that you be contacted regarding your son."

"My... my son?" Eli's thoughts careened away from Sheila to Noah, though he knew that couldn't be who the woman was referring to.

"Yes. Jacob McNamara. Your son."

"I don't have..." Eli wanted to deny that whoever this boy was, he wasn't his son, but something held his tongue. Clearly, there was no other parent in this boy's life if they believed that Eli was his father. And if Sheila was dead, Jacob was alone wherever he and Sheila had lived.

Eli decided it would be better to not deny parentage right at that moment. They could sort that out later with a simple DNA test. However, he didn't want to set the boy on a path that could end with him in foster care, especially when he did have family.

"What were you going to say?" the woman asked.

"I didn't know about a baby. Sheila never told me."

"I'm not sure how that's possible, since your name's on the birth certificate."

Eli had no answers for her, so he didn't offer any. "What do you need from me?"

"You'll have to come here to get Jacob. He's staying with a friend of his mom's at the moment, but that's not a permanent solution."

"Where is *here*?" Eli asked.

"Shreveport."

"Louisiana?"

"Yes."

"Okay. Can I have your name and number? I'll call you as soon as I have my travel plans in place."

Eli grabbed a pencil and his notebook, then jotted down the information. After the woman ended the call, Eli stared blankly at the floor of the workshop, the phone still gripped in his hand.

Following the revelation that Coral Thompson had hidden a letter from Sheila which revealed that she had run away, Eli had known that there was a possibility that Sheila might come back into his life one day. He just hadn't, in a million years, imagined it would be in this way.

His grief returned as he pictured Sheila as he'd once known her. Laughing and full of life. He'd loved her at one time, and though that love was no longer there in his heart, he still felt sadness over Sheila's death.

"Eli?"

He lifted his head and saw Anna leaning against the frame of the workshop door. She had her arms crossed, concern on her tired features.

"Hey. Why aren't you sleeping? Noah's still napping," he said, gesturing to the monitor that showed Noah's slumbering form on its screen.

"I heard your phone ring."

"Oh. Sorry about that." He looked down at his phone, trying to figure out how to share what the call had been about.

"Bad news?"

"Yeah. Sheila Thompson is dead."

"What?"

"I got a call from Shreveport, Louisiana, telling me that Sheila is dead."

"Why would they call you?" she asked. "Did she list you as next of kin or something?"

"Or something," Eli murmured. "She had a son and somehow managed to list me as his father."

Anna's sharp intake of breath wasn't unexpected. But when she didn't say anything more, Eli looked up.

"I don't understand," she said, her brow furrowed. "I thought you told me that you didn't sleep with her."

"I didn't." Eli frowned when Anna's expression didn't clear. "I'm not the boy's father."

"Then why would she say that you were?"

"I don't know." Eli tried to keep his aggravation from spilling over, knowing that his mindset wasn't being helped by his own lack of sleep.

It wasn't Anna's fault that he had been blindsided by the news and had no idea what was going on. He rubbed a hand over his face, struggling to figure out how best to deal with the situation. "I need to book a ticket to Shreveport."

"If he's not your son, why are you going?"

Like him, Anna was struggling with a lack of sleep, so Eli told himself that was why she didn't immediately understand why he had to go. These days, both of them seemed to reach the point of aggravation far more quickly than they ever had before.

"He's a boy who's just lost his mother," Eli said. "Even if he's not mine, he's a Thompson, and he has family here."

"Why can't they go get him, then?" she asked.

Eli's shoulders slumped as he felt torn in two different directions. Part of him agreed that he shouldn't have to be the one to go get the boy. However, he had a feeling that the authorities would give him less hassle since his name was on the birth certificate, along with Sheila stating in her suicide note that she wanted her son with him.

There was a boy down in Louisiana who was grieving and probably confused and unsure what life held for him. And yet, the woman he loved was struggling with her emotions, and there was a cranky baby who needed him too.

He owed Sheila nothing. They'd broken up before she'd left town, and the boy most definitely wasn't his son. So why did he feel so strongly about going to get him? Especially when he knew that Anna didn't want him to go?

"I promise I won't be gone long. Just a quick trip down there to get him and bring him back. It doesn't sound like there are any legal issues, so I'll probably just have to spend one night away. I'll ask Sarah to come stay with you and Noah."

Anna didn't say anything, and Eli dropped his gaze to his hands and the phone he still clutched. His heart ached as he considered that there was a child he could help, if even for just a short time, until they got the situation sorted out with the Thompsons. For sure, they'd want to know their nephew and grandson.

It was hard to ignore that there was a boy all alone who had just tragically lost his mom. Who had lived his life thinking his father didn't want him. Eli certainly wasn't his father, though the boy undoubtedly thought he was. But using the tenuous legal rights he currently had, he could bring Jacob home to the Thompson family.

He looked up and saw that Anna was no longer in the doorway. Immediately, he pushed to his feet and left the workshop, carrying the baby monitor with him. He prayed that Noah wouldn't wake up before they could get this issue settled, because trying to have any sort of discussion while the baby fussed was nearly impossible.

After checking a couple of places, he found Anna curled up on her side of their bed, facing the window that looked out over the forest. Her eyes were open, but he had a feeling that she wasn't seeing anything.

Eli got onto the bed with her, curling his body around hers and wrapping his arm over her waist. She held herself stiffly, like she was afraid to relax against him. Her smiles had become rare since Noah was born, and the connection that had been so strong between them felt like it was being stretched super thin. He just prayed it didn't snap.

"I love you," he said as he pressed his forehead to the back of her head, inhaling the familiar scent of her shampoo. "I don't want to leave you right now, but I feel like I need to do this. Not for Sheila, but for the boy who has lost everything."

"I don't want you to leave." Her voice was tight and low.

"I know that, sweetheart. But it will just be two days, and you know Sarah will be happy to stay with you. I'll be back before you know it. I promise."

She didn't relax in his arms like he'd hoped she would. Lately, she just seemed to always be tense. He wanted her to be able to relax and let him take her stress from her, if even for a little while. But now he was adding stress to her life by going away for a couple of days.

He wished she'd go back to sleep, but he knew that wasn't going to happen. So he just held her, not knowing what else to do, and prayed that God would help him be what Anna needed, even as he navigated this situation with Sheila's son.

All too soon, Noah began to fuss. Anna's body tensed even more, but before she could respond to the baby's cries, Eli pressed a kiss to her head.

"I'll get him. You stay here."

She didn't say anything more as Eli slipped off the bed and went to Noah's room. He knew that she loved their little boy with every bit of her being, but something was stressing her out, and the happy woman she'd been before getting pregnant was nowhere to be found.

The first few days following Noah's birth, she had seemed okay, relieved to finally not be dealing with a pregnancy that had been more difficult than she'd anticipated. She'd been tired, sure, but basically happy. But then colic had arrived, and most days she'd cried right alongside Noah. Smiles and laughter were not a part of their days much anymore.

Going into the nursery, he picked Noah up and cradled him to his chest.

"Didn't feel like sleeping a bit longer, huh?" Eli lifted him to his face and brushed a kiss across his cheek.

After checking to make sure he didn't need a diaper change, Eli left the nursery and walked downstairs to the living room. At six months, Noah was sitting up on his own, but Eli put him into the Exersaucer they had for him, then went to the kitchen to get one of the teethers that Anna kept in the freezer.

Once Noah was relatively settled, fussing a bit but seeming to be content to chew on the teether, Eli sat on the floor next to him, letting out a long breath. As he tried to entertain Noah with the toys on the Exersaucer, Eli mulled over what he needed do.

Finally, he pulled his phone out and called Sarah. As the big brother, he was used to being the one to take care of Leah and Sarah's problems, though that had lessened considerably as they'd each found the man who now offered them the support they needed. It felt odd to be calling on one of them to help him, but it was for Anna's sake.

Leah was currently on her honeymoon with her husband, Gavin, so that left Sarah. Although, even if Leah had been there, he'd still call Sarah first. Anna loved both of his sisters, but he knew she'd feel more comfortable having Sarah there in his absence.

"Hey, Eli!" Sarah answered with a cheerful note in her voice. "What's up?"

"Are you busy?" he asked.

"Not really." She spoke more slowly, as if hearing something in his words that worried her. "What do you need?"

"Can you come to the house? I need to ask you a huge favor."

"Sure. I'll be there in fifteen minutes."

"Thanks."

After the call ended, Eli stayed on the floor with Noah, doing his best to make the baby smile, though his own heart was heavy. He ran his hand over Noah's curls. The little guy had inherited Eli's dark hair, but his features were a mix of him and Anna, and every time Eli looked at him, love spilled over for both Noah and Anna.

Before he'd met Anna, there had been plenty of times that he'd thought he'd live the rest of his life alone. He hadn't wanted to be around people. Hadn't wanted to have to interact with people in a way that would allow him to meet that special someone. But then Anna had dropped into his life in a most unexpected way, and he couldn't help but be grateful that his aunt had sent her to the lodge, even though they'd been closed for renovations. She'd brought so much joy and love into his life since their first meeting.

Her job as a content creator for social media had continued to keep her busy over the past couple of years. She'd even documented a bit of her pregnancy, doing photo shoots of pregnancy styles, with Eli often helping her from behind the camera.

But as her pregnancy progressed, she hadn't posted as much, and what she did post seemed to lack the... effervescence of her earlier videos. Lately, he'd read through some comments on her Instagram posts where people had expressed concern that something had happened because she had hardly posted since Noah's birth.

He'd been glad to see her address their concerns by saying that she was just taking more time to enjoy being a mom... even though that didn't seem to be one hundred percent the truth. He just wanted her to find joy in her life once again.

When he heard a vehicle pull up outside, he got to his feet and went to the door to meet Sarah. He let her in, accepting the tight hug she gave him before going to see Noah.

After she'd loved on his son for a minute, she turned to look at him, hands on her hips. "You look terrible. What's going on?"

Eli walked to his favorite chair and sank down in it, while Sarah settled on the floor next to Noah. There was so much going on, but he wasn't going to divulge all the worries he had about Anna right then. He didn't think Anna would appreciate it.

So, instead, he dove right into the story about Sheila and her son.

"You *want* to go get him?" Sarah asked.

"I do. He has no one else, Sarah. And it's likely that they'll give anyone else hassles about taking him. Sheila somehow got me listed on the birth certificate and expressed her desire that I take custody of him. For his sake, I want to bring him back here, then I'll work with Pete and Josie to figure out how to give one of them custody."

Sarah seemed to consider his words while she waved a toy for Noah to grab. After a minute, she said, "I suppose that's probably the best thing to do. Poor child with no one else. He must be so confused. How old is he?"

Eli shrugged. "I'm not sure. They only told me his name."

"So what do you need from me?" she asked, glancing over at him.

He looked in the direction of the bedroom to make sure that Anna hadn't gotten up. "I was wondering if you'd be willing to stay with Anna while I'm gone. Noah's been quite cranky, and it's been taking two of us to keep up, one to take care of him so that the other can sleep."

Sarah's expression brightened. "Sure. I can do that. No problem. Can Beau come too?"

"The more the merrier," Eli said. "You can sleep in the spare room."

"When do you plan to leave?"

"I'd like to get a ticket out tomorrow so I can be back before the weekend."

"If you want, I can hang around while you get it all organized. Have you told Mom and Leah yet?"

Eli shook his head. "I wanted to see if you could stay with Anna before I said anything. I don't even know if Pete or Josie have been contacted about Sheila's death yet."

Sadness robbed the smile from Sarah's face. "I'd always hoped that she hadn't been killed, that she'd run away, which I guess is what happened. But committing suicide? I never would have thought she'd do that."

In the weeks before Sheila had left, her moods had been all over the place. Anger had been her most prevalent emotion, however, and Eli hadn't known what to make of it. Now, though, considering what had happened with Coral, Eli wondered if Sheila had already been struggling with mental health issues back then.

Whenever he'd thought of Sheila over the years—which admittedly hadn't been often recently—he'd hoped that if she was still alive, that she was happy. Now he'd never know for sure what she'd been through. But whatever it was, it must have not brought her happiness since she'd chosen to take her own life and leave her child an orphan.

A child that Eli was going to have to help through these first few days of grief. He wasn't sure he was qualified to do that, so he prayed that God would give him what he needed to comfort the boy.

CHAPTER THREE

Jacob wrapped his arms more tightly around his legs, tugging them closer so he could rest his chin on his knees. He stared intently at the closed door that led to the hallway outside the apartment, trying to ignore how his guts were shaking.

The knock had come five minutes ago, and Lynn had glanced at Jacob before going to answer the door. He'd known who was there. Someone had called earlier that morning to let him know that his father was on his way to collect him, but they hadn't told Lynn when he'd be there for certain. Just sometime later that afternoon.

Lynn had let Bobby stay home from school with him, and they'd played game after game of Fortnite, Jacob on Bobby's Switch, and Bobby on his Xbox. Though Jacob was usually better than Bobby at the game, he'd had a hard time focusing and kept getting eliminated, leaving Bobby to try to win the game.

He hadn't been able to eat any of the pizza Lynn had ordered, which he'd felt bad about because he was sure that she'd only bought it to make him feel better. Unfortunately, Jacob wasn't sure that anything would ever make him feel better.

And right then, he was waiting to meet his father, wondering what was being said out in the hallway between Lynn and the man. He'd barely gotten a glance at him when Lynn had opened the door.

"We can still play together once you get to wherever your dad lives, right?" Bobby asked, his brow furrowed. His blue eyes were wide with concern behind his glasses.

Jacob shrugged. "If he has an Xbox, I guess. If he doesn't..."

If he didn't, he'd lose contact with his best friend. His only friend. Jacob swallowed hard against the thought. *Please, God, let him be a nice man.* His mom had insisted that he was. But it had been a long time since she'd last seen him, so maybe he'd changed.

The fear that had flooded him when he'd been told that his father was coming to get him, continued to grow until Jacob was sure he was going to drown in it. What if he was mean? Jacob knew he was small for his age—the kids in his class constantly reminded him of that—and he'd be no match for a grown man if he got physical with him.

Nausea rose up within him, and saliva flooded his mouth. Scared he was going to throw up, Jacob scrambled off the couch and raced for the bathroom.

He heard Bobby yelling for his mom as he leaned over the toilet and retched. Nothing but liquid spilled out of him, and his body shook with the effort.

"Jacob, honey?"

He felt gentle hands touch him on the back, and tears burned his eyes at the knowledge that they didn't belong to his mom. His legs gave out and his arms couldn't support him, so he slumped to the floor.

"Let me get him," a man's voice said, deep and calm. The hands that lifted him from the floor were strong, but the movements were gentle.

Jacob took rapid breaths as he was carried from the bathroom, trying not to retch again and also trying to keep the sobs that wanted to escape from getting free. He couldn't let himself start to cry or he'd never stop, he was sure of it.

The man set him on the couch, then Jacob felt a cold cloth press against his face. He reached up to hold it over his eyes, afraid to look at the man and see disgust on his face. No man wanted a son that got so scared he threw up.

"What happened, Bobby?" Lynn asked.

"I don't know, Mom. We were sitting here talking about us still being able to play video games together, then he said maybe he wouldn't have an Xbox so we wouldn't be able to. Next thing, he's running for the bathroom."

Jacob shrank back against the couch, drawing his legs up again. He pulled his arms in tight against his body and pressed the cloth more tightly against his eyes as he rested his forehead on his knees.

A hand softly smoothed his hair. Jacob didn't know who it was, and he really didn't care because he knew for certain who it *wasn't*. And it was *her* touch that he longed for more than anything.

"I'm sure he's been through a lot," the man said. "It's not uncommon to have a physical reaction to an emotional upset."

"Are you taking him away?" Bobby asked.

"I have come to take him home with me, yes."

"Do you live close? Can I still see him? He's my best friend."

"I'm sorry, buddy. I live in Washington State, but I'll make sure that he's able to keep in contact with you, okay? And maybe we can arrange visits for the two of you in the future."

"Really?" Jacob felt someone bump his shoulder. "Did you hear that, Jake? He said we can still talk and see each other."

Jacob nodded but didn't lift his head. For some reason, the idea of looking at this man made him feel sick. Like it would make everything so much more real. Even more real than returning to the apartment that morning to pack up his stuff had felt.

"Do you have other kids?" Bobby asked.

"Yes. I have a son named Noah. He's six months old."

"Are you married to his mom?"

"Bobby!" Lynn admonished.

"Sorry, Mom."

"It's okay," the man said. "I don't mind answering. I'm sure you'd like to know about where Jacob is going. To answer your question, yes, I am married to his mom, Anna. We've been married for just over two years."

"Do you have an Xbox?" Bobby asked.

"I don't, but if that will help you two stay in touch, I'll see what I can do about getting one for Jacob."

Jacob took shallow breaths as he listened to the conversation around him. He wanted to believe what the man was saying because if it was true, it would mean he wouldn't be completely cut off from Bobby. He may have lost his mom, but he hoped that he didn't have to lose his best friend, too.

"Jacob, honey," Lynn said. "Would you like to meet Eli?"

Jacob gathered his limbs closer to his body and shook his head. It made no sense. He knew that. But somewhere in his mind, something was telling him that once he saw the man, the life he'd known would be officially over.

"It's okay," the man said. "I understand that this is difficult for him. Unfortunately, we do need to leave tomorrow. Our flight is scheduled to depart just before three p.m. I'll have to pick him up around one."

"How about we meet you at the airport?" Lynn suggested. "I can get him there on time."

"Sure. That would be fine."

"Can I stay home from school again, Mom?"

"Yes, darling. You can come to the airport with us."

Jacob now knew how many hours he had left in the place he considered his second home, his actual home having been emptied of the little that was his.

"Are there things of Jacob's that need to be shipped?"

Lynn sighed. "No. Sheila didn't have much, and Jacob has already chosen the things of hers that he wants to keep. He has just one suitcase and his backpack to travel with tomorrow."

"If he changes his mind about anything tonight and it doesn't fit in his suitcase, just keep it here, and I'll make arrangements to have it shipped to Washington."

"Okay. Thank you."

Jacob felt the couch shift as his father got to his feet. A hand touched his shoulder. "I'll see you tomorrow, Jacob. If you need anything from me tonight, Lynn has my number. You can call or text me."

Jacob nodded without lifting his head. He couldn't imagine what he'd need from this stranger, but he knew his mom would expect him to respond.

Even after the man had left, Jacob couldn't seem to lift his head. He felt the press of a body next to his and knew that Bobby was sitting right up against his side. From what he could hear, Bobby was playing a game on his Switch. Bobby's dad didn't see him much, but he seemed to make up for that by buying him anything he wanted. Which is why Bobby had both a Switch and an Xbox.

Jacob latched onto the idea that he might finally have an Xbox of his own. Even if it wasn't the latest model, he'd be happy with it, since it would mean he could still talk to Bobby. That little bit of happiness, however, didn't ease the pain and sadness that had taken up permanent residence in his heart and brain.

He wasn't sure that he'd ever be fully happy again.

CHAPTER FOUR

Eli fought the urge to pace in front of the check-in counter as he waited for Lynn to show up with Jacob. She'd assured him they'd be there, and he was early, so it was understandable why they hadn't arrived yet.

He just wanted to get home. When he'd called Anna the night before, they hadn't talked long since she had been trying to get Noah down. He'd told her to give the baby monitor to Sarah for the night so that she could get some solid sleep, but he doubted that she'd done that. Even though he'd only been gone a short time, he missed her and Noah, and just wanted to be with them again.

His introduction to Jacob definitely hadn't gone as planned. Seeing Jacob so distressed had made him angry at Sheila for leaving her son the way she had. Surely she had to have known how upset he'd be over her death.

Seeing the teen—he'd found out Jacob was thirteen, though he didn't look it—so upset the day before had been difficult. Jacob's grief had been palpable, and Eli had felt a powerful urge to take care of him in much the same way he cared for Noah when he was upset.

After that encounter, Eli had faced an unfortunate truth. They might not have had any sort of prior relationship, but he realized that Jacob was anticipating that he'd have a home with Eli now. The moment he told Jacob he wasn't really his dad, the teen was going to suffer another loss.

It made him realize that coming to get Jacob without revealing to him that Sheila had lied, had complicated the situation. Why had he thought it would be a simple thing? Now, in addition to an exhausted wife and an often-cranky baby, he had a teen who was broken by his mom's death and who thought Eli was his father.

Eli felt like he didn't have the energy or the ability to give his immediate family or Jacob what each of them needed. For the first time since he'd met Anna, Eli worried that he wouldn't be enough for her. That no matter what he did, it wouldn't be enough for any of them.

Pushing aside those thoughts to deal with later, Eli glanced over the crowd once again. Finally, he spotted Lynn moving toward him with the two boys.

As they approached him, Eli got his first good look at Jacob, taking in the way his clothes swam on his thin frame. His dark blond hair hung in messy curls almost to his shoulders, and Eli wondered if the long hair was a preference or if his mom hadn't had money to take him for haircuts. He wasn't going to push Jacob to change anything, but he did think they'd need to get him clothes that fit better.

Jacob's gaze, when it finally met Eli's, was filled with apprehension. Eli wished there was something he could say or do to assure the teen that he wasn't being turned over to someone who would abuse him, or worse. All he could do was show the boy that he was safe and that he would take care of him.

For a moment, Eli wondered why he was thinking of caring for Jacob in the long-term. That wasn't what he had told Anna they'd be doing. However, that had been before he'd met Jacob.

"Jacob," Lynn said, drawing up the suitcase she was pulling so that it sat beside her. "This is Eli."

Jacob continued to stare at him, his blue eyes dominating his thin face. "Hi."

"It's nice to meet you, Jacob," Eli said. "Though I'm sorry it's under these circumstances."

Jacob gave a tense nod, his hands clutching the straps of his backpack.

"I hope we're not late," Lynn said.

"We've got time, though I should probably get us checked in."

It took a few minutes, but Eli got their luggage and tickets sorted, and then they were free to wander the airport until closer to the time when they needed to go through security to proceed to their gate. The boys stuck close together while Lynn walked next to Eli.

"I worry about him," Lynn said softly. "I don't think he slept at all last night."

"I'm sure he's nervous about what's to come. I wish I didn't have to take him away from his life here, but I don't have a choice."

"He knows. It's just so much happening to him in such a short time."

"I understand. Bobby is welcome to contact him any time. Just call my cell phone number for the time being."

"Thank you for not cutting them off. I know Bobby is going to miss him tremendously, but he'll still be in a familiar place. It's Jacob I'm worried about."

"I know there's nothing I can say to alleviate that worry completely, but I'm going to try my best to help Jacob through this difficult time in his life."

Lynn gave him a small smile. "I suppose that's all I can hope for. It was probably all Sheila hoped for, too."

Eli thought of the letter from Sheila tucked into his bag. Lynn had given it to him the day before, along with one to be given to Jacob at a later date, probably assuming he'd read it the previous night. However, he hadn't been able to bring himself to open it just yet. His thoughts regarding Sheila were a bit of a mess, considering how negatively her actions had impacted his life.

But hearing that she'd killed herself... He wasn't sure if he wanted to read her suicide note to him. Not when he was struggling with so much himself at that moment.

When it came time to go through security, Eli swallowed hard against the emotion that welled up inside him when Jacob and Bobby hugged. Lynn finally had to pry them apart after swiping at the tears on her own cheeks. Gently resting his hand on Jacob's shoulder, Eli said goodbye to Lynn and Bobby, then guided him toward the security they'd need to pass through before going to their gate.

Jacob walked with his head bent, following Eli's instructions as they made their way to their gate. Once there, Eli found them a couple of empty seats, then sat with his arm across the back of Jacob's seat. A huge part of him wanted to gather the boy close and let him cry out the heartache he was sure had taken up residence inside him, but he was a stranger to Jacob.

Instead, he reached into his carry-on and pulled out the tablet he'd brought with him. It was already set up to use the hotspot on his phone.

"I don't have any games on this," he said as he unlocked it and brought up the app store. "But if you want to download some, you can."

Jacob turned his head to stare at the tablet for a moment before he glanced up at Eli then took it from him. He seemed to know what he was doing as he typed something into the search bar. When the results came up, he tapped one game, its information filling the screen.

Jacob turned it so Eli could see it. "Lynn lets us play this on her phone."

Eli smiled as he recognized the game. "Anna likes to play that one, too. Go ahead and get it."

It took only a moment for the game to download, then Jacob began to play it, starting at level one. Though Eli wasn't sure what sort of games Jacob usually played, he was glad that to start with, he wasn't having to restrict an inappropriate game.

When their flight began to board, Jacob's eyes went wide when they got up to board with the first-class passengers. Eli didn't travel much, but in the few trips he'd taken with Anna, he'd come to realize that because of his height, he was far more comfortable with extra legroom. Plus, he didn't want the two of them squeezed into a row with a stranger who might want to make conversation.

He didn't think either of them was ready for that.

Eli guided Jacob into the seat by the window, noticing how the larger seat swamped the boy. He settled down beside him, then instructed Jacob on how to buckle himself in.

Jacob looked from the window to the people streaming onto the plane, then back to the window again. It seemed pretty clear that this was his first time flying, though Eli didn't ask him to confirm that.

Once they were in the air, Jacob stared out the window for a while, but then turned his attention back to the tablet. When the flight attendant offered them drinks, he asked for a soda while Eli got a coffee.

It was a short flight, barely giving them time to finish their drinks before their cups were collected. Once on the ground in Houston, they had just over an hour before they had to board their next flight. Eli stopped to grab them some food since he wasn't sure what they'd be served on the plane, and he'd rather get something Jacob would eat.

It was a longer stretch from Houston to Seattle, and after about an hour in the air, Jacob fell asleep. Eli blew out a breath in relief. The boy had barely said more than a handful of words to him so far, but he could see the strain and exhaustion on him.

Since Eli wasn't the chattiest person around, he hadn't pushed Jacob to talk, and he hoped that wasn't a mistake. If this had all happened before Noah was born, he would have relied on Anna to help him communicate with Jacob because she was so much better at stuff like that. But now that she was caring for Noah and dealing with her own exhaustion, he didn't feel right asking for her help.

Jacob didn't wake up until the plane bounced on the runway in Seattle. His eyes flew open, and he straightened, panic clear on his face. It only eased when he saw Eli.

Eli covered Jacob's hand with his where it gripped the armrest between them. "It's okay. We've just landed in Seattle." He gave Jacob's hand a light squeeze before letting go. "I have my vehicle here, and it's about an hour's drive to New Hope."

"That's where your house is?" Jacob asked.

"Yes. My family actually owns a vacation resort with a lodge and cabins. Anna and I have a home on the same land, and I help my mom run the resort."

"And there's room for me?"

"Yes. You'll have a room of your own." He'd texted Sarah to ask if she'd change the sheets and prepare the room she and Beau had used for Jacob.

"Will I have to go to school?"

Eli could tell that he hoped the answer was no, but that just wasn't possible. "Yes. There's a school in New Hope. It's the same one I attended when I was your age."

"Did my mom go there too?"

"Yep, she did. So did my sisters and your mom's sister."

He still didn't know if anyone had informed Pete or Josie about Sheila's death. The social worker he'd dealt with had said that she'd only had Eli's information. Eli had questioned the worker about how they knew that she'd committed suicide and not been murdered. Aside from all the letters she'd left behind, she'd apparently called 911 to tell them of her intentions so that they would be the ones to find her and not Jacob.

Before he'd left Shreveport, Eli had made sure that the bill for the cremation Sheila had requested was covered and left his mailing address for shipment of her ashes. Maybe they could have a service for Sheila once things had settled down.

"Will I be able to meet my mom's sister?" Jacob asked. "Is she nice?"

"Yes, you can meet her, and she is very nice. She's a nurse."

Before Jacob could ask any more questions, the seatbelt sign went off. Eli and Jacob were able to disembark quickly. Once they had their bags, they walked to where Eli had parked his vehicle the previous day.

Eli opened the front passenger side door for Jacob, then put their bags in the back, pulling out the tablet again before shutting the rear hatch. As he slid behind the wheel, he glanced at the teen. He was staring out the front window, his arms crossed over his chest.

"Are you hungry?" Eli asked. It wasn't super late, and if the boy was willing to eat, Eli would be happy to feed him.

Jacob glanced at him, then shook his head.

"Okay. We've got about an hour's drive. If you change your mind, let me know." He handed Jacob the tablet. "You can play on that again if you want."

Jacob took it from him. "Thank you."

Eli considered calling Anna to chat on the way, but he still wasn't sure how she felt about Jacob. He didn't want to have a discussion about the teen with Jacob right there. Instead, he sent a quick text to let Sarah know that they'd landed and were on their way.

Then he turned on the radio and began the drive home, trying not to think too much about what the next few days might hold.

~*~

Sarah stared at the text from Eli on her phone. She was glad that he was on his way home, but worry gnawed at her. The past two days had been eye-opening, and not necessarily in a good way.

"Eli says they're just leaving the airport," Sarah said as she joined Anna in the living room.

The other woman looked up, her expression drawn and tired. "Okay."

Sarah had tried to feel the woman out for what her thoughts were on Jacob's arrival. All she'd said was that Jacob wouldn't be living with them for long. That Eli had said he would live with Josie or Pete.

Sarah wasn't sure that was going to happen. Something told her that Eli might not have thought of the logistics of the situation. Pete had no room for anyone, since Josie had mentioned that he'd recently moved into a one-bedroom apartment. And Josie herself was a live-in nurse, so that situation likely wouldn't allow for a child to live with her.

She didn't voice any of that to Anna, but she was going to have to talk to Eli about it sooner rather than later. And that wasn't the only thing she was going to talk to him about.

It seemed that Anna had managed to act like her usual self for the short periods of time they'd been together over the past six months. But after having stayed with her for almost forty-eight hours, Sarah could see that something was off.

Shortly after Noah's, they'd permanently changed the location of their Sunday evening Bible studies when Eli had said that it was becoming more challenging to have the studies there while they were adjusting to having a newborn baby. Given that none of the other attendees had kids—except for Michael and Lani Reed—they'd just accepted that there needed to be a change.

Sarah felt horrible that she hadn't picked up on anything before coming to stay with Anna. Granted, she wasn't around her nearly as much as she'd used to be. As Anna's pregnancy had progressed, she'd stepped back from much of the work around the lodge, and that had carried on after Noah's birth. So not seeing Anna as often hadn't made Sarah think that anything was wrong.

She'd also had stuff going on in her own life, as she'd been busy preparing for another art show. There had actually been a few days during that time when she'd barely seen Beau since she'd be working through the night. Now, though, seeing the strain on Anna's face, Sarah wished that she had sought her sister-in-law out more frequently.

Given that Eli had asked her to stay with Anna while he took his quick trip, Sarah hoped that was an indication that he was aware of what was going on with Anna. However, on the off chance that he was too close to the situation—and perhaps dealing with exhaustion himself—she was definitely going to bring her observations to his attention.

Her first instinct had been to call her mom and Leah and tell them what she was seeing, but she knew she needed to talk to Eli first. But not telling her twin and their mom what she suspected was the hardest thing she'd ever done—or not done, as the case may be.

CHAPTER FIVE

Anna fitted Noah into the sling in his preferred position, then exhaled heavily. He was settled for the time being, but she knew it wouldn't last. It never did. And when he got really fussy, he was inconsolable. Nothing she did would soothe him.

It seemed like everything she'd believed about motherhood had been wrong. The overwhelming happiness she'd thought she'd experience at the birth of their son was absent. Too often, feelings of inadequacy and sadness filled her days.

On top of that, she was exhausted... always so very tired. There were days she just wanted to fall asleep and not wake up for a year. Maybe by then Noah would be happier, and she'd be a better mother.

When she considered that her mom had had her and still kept going to work without taking much time off at all, it made her feel like there was something wrong with her. Even Nadine, Eli's mom, had managed to run the lodge after having twins.

And yet there she was, unable to get through a day without crying. All she had to do was care for her son and make a video or post a couple of times a week on her social media, and she couldn't even manage that.

"Eli says they're just leaving the airport."

Anna looked up as Sarah joined her in the living room. "Thank you."

She could see concern on Sarah's face, but thankfully, she didn't say anything more. Though she would rather have had Eli with her, she was grateful that she hadn't been alone while he was gone. The thought of being completely on her own with Noah for such an extended stretch of time had scared her a bit.

During the day, if Eli was gone, she was always a nervous wreck until he came home. She wasn't sure why she felt that way, except that it seemed better to have two of them there if Noah got upset. That way, they could spell each other off.

Though Sarah had offered to listen for the baby during the night, Anna hadn't taken her up on that. What kind of mother would let someone other than the baby's father take care of the baby through the night? It felt like announcing to the world that she was struggling.

And she didn't even want to think about the situation that would unfold once Eli got home. Sarah had said that she was changing the sheets so the room was ready for the boy arriving with Eli, which had made everything more real.

She'd tried not to think about the reason why Eli had been gone for the past two days. He'd told her back before they'd gotten married that he'd never had a physical relationship with Sheila, and he'd reiterated that before he'd left. And yet he was bringing home a boy who had a birth certificate stating differently.

Anna didn't know how Sheila had managed it, but it was hard not to allow the little kernel of doubt over what Eli had told her to take root. It seemed like the worst time in the world for this to be happening.

But would there ever have been a good time for something like this? Anna wasn't sure there was. At least not for her.

"Have a cookie," Sarah said, holding out one of the large double chocolate chip cookies that Beau had brought with him when he'd come from work the previous day. "Want a glass of milk?"

"You don't need to do that," Anna said, hating how she wasn't even able to entertain guests properly in her own home.

Sarah gave her a quick smile. "Beau's pouring me a glass of cold milk. Would you like one too?"

"Sure. Thanks."

She could drink milk now that she wasn't nursing anymore. It was one of the things that she tried cutting out of her diet, hoping to help Noah not be so fussy anymore. As it turned out, eliminating milk from her diet hadn't made any difference. And though she'd wanted to nurse Noah more than anything, she'd ended up weaning him for several reasons. They might have all been valid, but that hadn't made her feel any better about having to stop.

When Sarah returned with two glasses of milk, she handed one to Anna. "Cookie with milk. The perfect snack. Too bad you can't have any, baby Noah."

She ran her fingers lightly over Noah's curls, and Anna held her breath, hoping it wouldn't be something that would set him off. Thankfully, he only turned his eyes briefly in Sarah's direction before he went back to sucking on his pacifier.

Sighing in relief, Anna broke off a piece of a cookie and ate it. The cookie really was quite good, but she only had a moment to enjoy it. Noah let out a squeak and began to squirm, and as the pacifier fell onto the floor, the squeak turned into fussing.

"Let me take him for a bit," Sarah said, setting aside her cookie. "I haven't gotten to hold him enough. Especially if I want to be his favorite aunt."

Anna wanted to protest that she could take care of him. But honestly, she wasn't sure she could. At her nod, Sarah came and helped free Noah from the wrap. He continued to fuss even as Sarah rocked him, and Anna clenched her hands, fighting the urge to take him back.

"What's wrong, little guy?" Sarah crooned, gently bouncing and swaying as she held Noah close. "You need to learn to talk so that you can tell us what's up."

Anna had often had a similar thought herself. She felt like she was an idiot because she couldn't seem to figure out Noah's cries so she could soothe him and meet his needs. She was his mother. Why was it so hard for her to do what should come naturally?

Beau came from the kitchen with another glass of milk and a plate of cookies. He set them down on the coffee table, then went to his wife and leaned down to speak to Noah.

Watching them, Anna realized that they had more joy in interacting with Noah than she seemed to. A knot of anxiety tightened in her gut. What was wrong with her?

She worried over that thought as she tried to eat the cookie without gagging and to drink most of the milk. It was only when lights swept through the living room window that another worry took its place.

"Looks like Eli's home," Beau said as he headed for the front door.

Anna watched as he opened the door and disappeared outside. Sarah kept Noah, though she got up from where she'd settled on the couch earlier with Beau.

It only took a couple of minutes before Beau reappeared with a suitcase. Behind him came Eli with the boy he'd gone to pick up. Sheila's son.

"Hey there," Beau said after he set the bag down. "I'm Beau."

The boy looked up at Beau from beneath a mess of curly dark blond hair. Anna wasn't sure what she'd expected, but the painfully thin boy who stood next to Eli wasn't it.

"This is Jacob," Eli said, resting his hand on Jacob's shoulder. "Jacob, Beau is my brother-in-law. He's married to my sister, Sarah, who is the one holding Noah over there."

Anna finally got to her feet, knowing it would be expected of her to welcome him, regardless of how she felt about the whole situation.

"Hi, Jacob," Sarah said as she moved over to where he and Eli still stood. "It's nice to meet you."

Jacob's eyes seemed impossibly large in his narrow face as he nodded at her. He looked uncomfortable and a little scared. Anna felt badly for him. Hopefully, he'd be settled with his family soon.

"And this is my wife, Anna," Eli said, guiding Jacob closer to where she stood. "Anna, this is Jacob."

She wasn't sure if the boy would shake her hand if she held it out, so she just said, "Welcome, Jacob."

"Thank you." His voice was soft, and he only met her gaze briefly before staring back down at the floor.

"I'm sure you're tired," Eli said. "So why don't I show you where your room is?"

Jacob nodded, clutching at the straps of his backpack.

"I'll be right back." Eli picked up the suitcase, then gestured for Jacob to follow him upstairs to the bedroom where Beau and Sarah had slept the night before.

"How old did Eli say he was?" Sarah asked after they'd disappeared up the stairs.

"Thirteen, I think," Anna replied.

"I'm not a good judge of teen boys, but he looks really small for thirteen."

"I was thin like that as a teen, though I was taller," Beau said. "He might just be a little late with his growth spurts."

Anna didn't want to feel concerned or worried about the boy when she already had so much on her mind, so she went to Sarah and held out her arms for the baby. "I suppose you two probably want to get on home."

Sarah sighed and handed Noah back with apparent reluctance. "Yeah. I need to do some painting tonight. I will be back, however, for more baby cuddles in the near future."

Anna wasn't sure if she wanted that or not, but she just nodded as she shifted Noah into her arms. Almost immediately he began to fuss, and she bounced gently in hopes he'd settle down.

Sarah gave her a long look before turning to Beau. "Take me home, husband!"

Beau smiled down at her, then took her hand. "Talk to you later, Anna."

Anna watched the two go, trying to remember the last time she and Eli had been so lighthearted with each other. It felt like an eternity. As Noah's fussing turned to whimpers, which she knew were a precursor to outright crying, tears pricked at the back of her eyes. She wasn't sure she'd be able to keep from crying if Noah started.

"Hey there, little guy," Eli said as he approached them from the direction of the stairs. One of his arms went around her, and he cupped Noah's head with his hand. "And hello to you too, sweetie. I missed you."

A lump in her throat almost prevented her response. "Missed you too."

"Why don't you go get ready for bed?" he said. "I'll take care of getting Noah his bottle and putting him down."

Anna felt guilty for taking him up on the offer, considering he was coming back from a trip, but she desperately needed sleep.

"Are you sure?"

"I'm positive." Eli bent to press a light kiss to her lips. "Go to bed and get some sleep."

"Okay. Thank you."

Eli pulled her and Noah close for a second, then took the baby from her. She turned toward their room, eager to sleep and escape all the negative emotions that clung to her in a way she couldn't seem to get away from while awake.

Where she once would have spent time on her nighttime skin-care routine, Anna just brushed her teeth and changed into her pajamas. She avoided looking at herself in the mirror while she was in the bathroom, afraid of what she'd see.

Back in the bedroom, she climbed under the blankets and turned off the light. In the past, she would have gravitated to the middle of the bed so that she could cuddle with Eli. That night, however, she stayed close to the edge on her side.

Sleep was all she craved anymore. No nighttime cuddles and whispered words of affection. No physical intimacy. Just sleep.

Eli seemed to understand. But how long would he be okay with the situation? It was just one more thing she was failing at. One more pressure that seemed to want to smash her right into the ground.

As she lay in the semi-darkness, having left the small lamp on Eli's side of the bed on, Anna struggled to fall asleep.

As usual, her thoughts were her enemy, circling round and round. Never settling. Tears pricked at her eyes as frustration filled her. She was *so* tired. How come her body wouldn't just do this one thing right and let her sleep?

Hot tears slid down her cheeks. What was she supposed to do? How was she supposed to get the rest she needed? If she didn't fall asleep soon, she'd be useless when Noah woke in the night.

Finally, after what felt like forever, her body overrode her frantic thoughts and pulled her into the oblivion of sleep.

Eli walked the floor with Noah, praying as he paced that Noah would get to where he'd sleep more and be less fussy. That they'd figure out what would make their little guy more content.

He prayed for Anna, who he knew was overwhelmed with everything, pleading with God to give him wisdom on how to help her.

And he prayed for Jacob as he grieved the loss of his mom and the life he'd lived in Louisiana.

Then he prayed for himself because he was so worried that he would not be able to be the support that each of those he loved needed him to be.

When his phone beeped with a text, he almost ignored it. But after a few moments, he pulled it out to see who it was from.

Sarah: *Call me when you have a minute.*

After a brief hesitation, Eli tapped the screen to place the call. When Sarah answered, Eli said, "What's up?"

"Anna needs help."

Sarah's blunt statement had Eli frowning. "What?"

"I think she might have postpartum depression."

"What do you mean?"

"Eli, she's a shell of herself, and she seems so uncertain of everything when it comes to caring for Noah."

"She's just tired," Eli said, though now that the seed had been planted, he couldn't ignore it. "Noah really doesn't sleep well. He's still up through the night, and he doesn't like to nap during the day. Neither of us is getting much sleep."

"Talk to her doctor about it, Eli," Sarah said, her tone firm, which was quite unlike her. "Something's not right. I'm worried about her, and though I know it's not your or Jacob's fault, that whole situation isn't going to help her."

Eli knew that was probably true, but he didn't know what to do about it. "I don't usually go to her appointments, though."

"I'm just worried," Sarah said. "I've never seen her like this. I feel bad that I've been so busy I haven't been helping you like I should have been."

"We're not your responsibility, Sarah," Eli told her.

"I know that," Sarah said with a sigh. "But I love you guys, and I want to help. Unfortunately, Anna wouldn't let us take the baby monitor last night. It was like she was afraid that it would reflect poorly on her if she needed our help."

Eli held Noah close while he dragged his hand down his face. He'd gotten that feeling from Anna as well. He'd just thought it reflected the perfectionist part of her personality. But now, he could see that it might mean something more. Something bad.

"I'll call her doctor first thing on Monday morning." He was sure she was going to protest, but he couldn't take the chance of not getting her help if she needed it.

"Let me know when the appointment is, and I'll come by to watch Noah and Jacob."

"Thanks," Eli said with a sigh.

"Are you going to be at church tomorrow?"

Eli thought of Anna's weariness, Noah's fussiness, and Jacob's wariness and grief. "I think we'll probably just stick close to home and catch the service on the livestream. I still need to talk to Josie about what's happened."

"Why not Pete?"

"I think that Josie would be better able to handle the news, and she'd know how to break it to her dad." He thought of the letters in his bag. The one addressed to him that was still unopened. "I wish I didn't have to tell them that Sheila is dead."

"It seems unfair that you've been dragged back into the situation, considering all you've dealt with because of Sheila," Sarah agreed. "But I also think it's best Josie hear it from you. You'll deliver it with compassion because you know them."

Eli knew she was right, but it wasn't easy to be the bearer of such news. And he still needed to figure out what to do with Jacob. Right then, he had no idea what the best course of action was for the boy, especially if Sarah was right about Anna dealing with depression. Having Jacob there with them might not be a good idea.

He thought of the way Jacob had looked at him with a mixture of grief, fear, and just the tiniest bit of hope. It was that hope that Eli couldn't ignore. He knew that Jacob thought he was his father, and he wasn't sure he could find it within himself to dash his hopes and add to the grief he already felt.

"We'll be praying for you," Sarah said. "We love you guys so much."

Eli swallowed against the emotion that threatened to choke him. "Love you too. Thank you for praying."

After they ended the call, he slid his phone into his pocket, realizing then that Noah had settled. His eyes were closed, dark lashes fanning out across his chubby cheeks. His little fist rested on Eli's chest.

Love flooded Eli as he pressed a gentle kiss to Noah's curls. He couldn't help but think of the other boy who thought he was his father. How different their lives were. He was filled with a strong desire to give Jacob the same stable life he was providing for Noah.

But first, he needed to take care of Anna. She was his heart, and he couldn't do any of this without her. Plus, his love demanded that he fix whatever was wrong so that she smiled again without the weariness weighing her down.

With a final kiss to Noah's soft hair, Eli carefully settled him in his crib, leaving his hand on him for a minute before gently removing it. He stood staring at him, then turned and left the room, hoping that he'd sleep peacefully and give them all a break.

CHAPTER SIX

Anna stared at the glowing numbers of the clock on her nightstand. The next time Noah woke, she'd be up for the day. Beside her, Eli was asleep, and for a moment, she felt a surge of frustration. It wasn't fair that he could fall asleep so easily.

Even when he woke up with Noah's crying, as soon as the baby was settled again, Eli fell right back to sleep. Meanwhile, Anna's brain kicked into gear, and all she could seem to focus on was how long it would be until Noah woke up again. But knowing that she needed to fall asleep right away seemed to only make the problem worse.

Even pre-Noah, she'd never fallen asleep right away, but once she did, she usually stayed asleep. And if she didn't, she could still sleep in or take a nap if she needed to. Neither of those was really an option anymore, which left her in a state of chronic exhaustion.

In the quiet darkness of the room, her thoughts screamed at her. Pointing out every single thing she was failing at. Being a mother. Being a wife. Doing her job. There was no area in her life where she didn't feel like she was falling short.

Unfortunately, she had no idea how to get her life back on track. She'd been so excited about having a baby, but pregnancy hadn't been as easy as she'd hoped. Her labor had been long, but thankfully, the delivery had gone smoothly. The first couple of weeks had been okay as she'd recovered from the delivery and tried to learn how to breastfeed.

However, things had started to fall apart when Noah had ended up with colic. And months later, everything was still a mess. Thanksgiving was just around the corner, and then the holidays

would kick off. Usually, by Thanksgiving, she had already purchased most—if not all—of her presents, and she could just enjoy
the time leading up to Christmas.

That was definitely not the case this year. She hadn't even
thought about Christmas presents, let alone bought any. She really
wished that there was a fast-forward button so that she could just
jump to January. Christmas would be over, and maybe Noah would
have finally begun to sleep through the night.

Noah began to cry, drawing her from the quagmire of thoughts
that had kept her from falling back asleep. Anna pushed up to sit
on the edge of the bed, knowing she needed to get moving before
Noah woke Eli. There was no need for him to get up when she was
already awake.

She reached out and turned off the monitor, then made her way
out of the bedroom and up the stairs to Noah's room. The door to
Jacob's room was open a crack, but she didn't hear him moving
around.

In the nursery, she lifted Noah from the crib and carried him to
the change table to change his diaper before wrapping the sling
around them. When she reached the main floor, Shadow slowly
got up from his spot near Eli's workshop and came to bump his
nose against her leg in greeting.

It was still dark as she made her way to the kitchen, but strategi-
cally placed nightlights guided her steps. She flicked on the light,
then went to work getting a bottle ready for Noah. While it warmed
up, she dumped food into Shadow's bowl.

Through it all, Noah gurgled and waved his arms. Happy for
the moment, apparently. When the bottle was ready, she went to
the rocking chair in the living room.

She'd started using the sling when she fed him on the off chance
she zoned out or even dozed off slightly. The last thing she wanted
to do was to drop Noah. Thankfully, Noah was used to the sling,

and usually didn't fuss too much when he was in it, especially if he had his bottle.

He'd gotten through about half the bottle when movement in the hallway that led to the stairs drew Anna's attention. She looked over, expecting to see Eli. Instead, it was Jacob who hovered near the bottom of the stairs, his arms crossed over his chest.

Anna realized that it was two hours later in Shreveport, so it was possible he'd been awake for a little while already.

"Hi," she said, determining in that moment that maybe this was something she could manage not to fail at. She could be polite and welcoming for the short time he'd be spending with them.

Jacob ventured a little closer. "Hi."

"Are you hungry?" she asked.

He shook his head as he settled on the edge of the couch.

"Are you sure?" The boy looked like he could use a good meal. "There's cereal and milk. Or if you wait a bit, Eli or I can make you eggs or pancakes."

"Thank you, but I'm not hungry."

"Well, if you change your mind, you can eat whatever is in the kitchen." Something told her she didn't have to worry about him raiding their cupboards or fridge and leaving them empty.

"Thank you." His gaze lowered to Noah, and Anna wondered what was going through his mind as he studied the baby.

She had no idea what to say, and she wished Eli would wake up so he could take care of Jacob.

Shadow wandered into the living room, then approached Jacob. Anna hoped he wasn't scared of dogs, but it became quickly apparent that she needn't have worried. Jacob held out his hand for Shadow to sniff, then when the dog gave his fingers a lick, Jacob rubbed him behind his ears.

Being an older dog, Shadow wasn't one to overwhelm visitors. Sometimes he didn't even bother to get up off his favorite bed when they arrived. If he did, he was content to bump up against them and wait for them to give him pets and scratches. Jacob was currently his favorite person, if the way he was wagging his tail was any indication.

"What's his name?" Jacob asked.

"That's Shadow." The dog sat down in front of Jacob, his tail still wagging against the floor. "He loves people to pet him. Did you have a dog?"

Jacob shook his head. "We lived in an apartment, plus Mom..." His words trailed off for a moment. "Mom said we couldn't afford one."

Anna stared tiredly at the teen, taking in how he continued to pet Shadow. It was apparent that he liked animals. Or at least dogs. Shadow was a special dog. He didn't mind when Noah grabbed at his ears or his fur. Never growling or barking at the baby. They'd wondered how he might do when Noah first came home, but nothing about the baby seemed to bother the dog.

Even when Noah was crying and fussing for what seemed like hours, the dog simply lay there, his gaze following whoever was holding the baby as they paced the floor.

When Noah finished his bottle, he squirmed and try to adjust himself in her arms. Anna shifted around so he could see Jacob and Shadow.

Jacob glanced up, his gaze landing on the baby. The two seemed to engage in a friendly staring contest that was only broken when Noah let out a squeal and waved his arms.

"I think he's saying hi," Anna said.

"Does he talk?" Jacob asked, his gaze flicking to hers for a moment.

"Not yet. He babbles a lot but doesn't say any words."

Before she could say anything more, she heard footsteps and knew that Eli was up. When he appeared, he looked like he'd just rolled out of bed and tugged on his sweats and a T-shirt.

He paused, looking back and forth between the two of them. "You should have woken me. I would have gotten up with Noah."

"You'd already been up with him twice. It was my turn."

Noah let out another squeal and waved his arms in the air, obviously wanting his dad. Eli smiled and came over to where Anna sat with him. He bent down and gave her a kiss before taking Noah out of the sling.

"Why don't you go back to bed for a bit?" he said. "I've got this."

Anna was tempted. Even though Eli had gotten up with Noah through the night, she'd still woken up when he'd fussed.

"Go back to bed," he said again.

She wasn't sure that she'd be able to shut off her brain enough to fall asleep now that she was wide awake, but maybe she should try. Maybe her exhaustion would be stronger than her brain for once.

"Okay. If you're sure."

The smile he gave her was soft, yet edged with concern. "I'm very sure."

She nodded and got to her feet. She glanced at Jacob and found he was watching them with no expression on his face. Would he be gone when she woke up? Eli hadn't said when Sheila's family would come to pick him up.

It was probably difficult for the boy to go from one home to another and then another, but the sooner he was with one of the Thompsons, the sooner he'd be in his permanent home.

As Anna had suspected, it took forever to fall asleep, and it seemed that she had only just closed her eyes when the alarm she'd set went off. After she shut it off, she flipped onto her back and stared at the ceiling.

Why had she set that alarm? She should have just slept until she woke up on her own. Except that with how tired she felt most days, she might never have woken up.

Would that have been a bad thing?

Even as the thought crossed her mind, she shook it off. That wasn't like her. What was happening? Never in her life had she ever had thoughts like that.

Rolling over, she got out of bed and went to the bathroom. She took care of her business and washed up before leaving the room.

She felt so much like she was a stranger to herself these days. And that terrible thought had just added to that feeling.

Without the aid of the mirror, she smoothed her hair into a ponytail, then changed into a pair of leggings and a sweater. She still hadn't lost the weight she'd gained with Noah, which didn't make much sense as she wasn't eating all that much these days. Certainly not enough to warrant her jeans still being as tight as they were.

Taking a deep breath to fortify herself for whatever awaited her, Anna left the bedroom. She heard voices, and when she reached the living room, she saw that Nadine was there, sitting in the rocking chair.

Jacob was on the floor next to Noah in the Exersaucer. He was making the toys attached to the seat make noise or dance in a way that Noah couldn't do yet. The toy movements delighted the baby, making him smile and giggle.

For a moment, Anna felt the cloud over her lift as she watched her usually fussy baby smile and laugh. But just as quickly, it smothered her again because she knew that the happiness in Noah wouldn't last.

"Hello, darling," Nadine said as she came to where Anna stood.

The older woman hugged her tightly, and Anna allowed herself to relax into the embrace, appreciating the love Nadine had always showered on her. She was truly blessed to have her as a mother-in-law. She set the example for the type of mom Anna wanted to be.

Her own mom had taught her how to go after what she wanted and work hard for it, but she hadn't been a very affectionate parent, and neither was her dad. Anna hadn't realized what was missing from her life until she'd met the McNamaras. She wanted Noah to be surrounded by that love in a way that she hadn't been.

The problem was that even though she wanted that, her own body and emotions seemed to work against her. Most days, she felt incapable of giving Noah the type of love she wanted to.

"I hope you don't mind me coming by," Nadine said as she stepped back. "I brought food."

Anna trailed after her as she headed for the kitchen. Eli was already there, pulling plates and glasses out of the cupboard. He smiled when he saw her and put the dishes on the counter. After he gave her a kiss, he stared down at her.

"Did you get some sleep?"

The concern on his face weighed on her. It was an expression that seemed all too common these days. She didn't want him to be so worried.

"Yes. Thank you for letting me sleep. Do you want to go for a nap?"

Eli shook his head. "I'm gonna eat something, and then I need to go talk to Josie."

While Anna held no affection for Sheila or her mother, Coral, her heart went out to Josie. This news would not be easy for her to hear, especially if she had to be the one to tell her parents.

"Are you taking Jacob with you?"

"I don't think that would be a good idea. I'm not sure that springing the news of Sheila's death on Josie with Jacob present would be good for either of them."

Nadine took the plates to the table and began to set it. Anna picked the glasses up and followed her. Together they got the table ready, then Nadine went to the oven and pulled out a large casserole dish.

As they sat at the table a few minutes later, Anna was grateful for a meal that she hadn't had to cook. She hadn't been a super great cook when she'd met Eli, but over the past two years, Nadine and Leah had helped her improve. Still, these days, she appreciated when someone else did the cooking.

Jacob shifted in his chair, looking around at them when Eli said they were going to pray. Still, he bowed his head, which made Anna think that perhaps Sheila had shared her faith with her son.

"How was church today?" Eli asked as they began to eat.

Anna paused with a forkful of casserole on the way to her mouth. It was Sunday? How was she not keeping track of the days better?

As she ate, she listened to Nadine talk about the service. The worship team and the songs they'd sung. The sermon. The people she'd spoken to. Anna longed to be part of that again. Unfortunately, they missed more services than they attended recently, usually catching the livestream on the computer instead, since that required less effort.

It was a couple of hours before Eli left the house, and Anna could see the apprehension on his face. Nadine was still there, and she prayed with him before he left.

"He's so strong," Nadine said as she stood at the front window, watching Eli drive away. "But I'm sure this is tearing him up inside."

Anna knew she was right. His quiet strength was one of the things she'd been drawn to, and it was something she'd leaned on over the past several months. But even the strongest person could reach a breaking point. Would she be strong enough to support him if he got to that point?

In her current state, she wasn't sure.

CHAPTER SEVEN

Eli pulled the SUV over to the side of the road and brought it to a stop. Thankfully, the stretch that led away from the Hawkins' mansion was fairly deserted, so he didn't have to worry about any traffic.

After putting his vehicle in park, he slumped back against the seat and closed his eyes. Informing Josie about the death of her sister had taken a toll on him. Selfishly, he was glad he didn't have to be the one to tell Pete and Coral.

Josie hadn't been super close to her older sister, and in a lot of ways, Sheila hadn't treated Josie very well. When she hadn't been outright ignoring her, Sheila was telling her she was a pest. A pain in the neck.

Eli knew what it was like to have younger siblings—though the age spread hadn't been as big between him and the twins—but he'd never treated them the way Sheila had treated Josie. He'd tried to talk to her about the relationship, but in the months before she left, Sheila had been angry and resentful, unwilling to listen to anyone. Not her mom. Not her dad. And certainly not Eli.

He had never imagined that this would be how things would end for Sheila. He'd finally read the letter she'd addressed to him, and though it had broken his heart to read about all that had happened to her after she left New Hope, it also explained so much. It had left him with conflicted feelings about Jacob, however.

The sadness that had permeated Sheila's letter, and her feelings of not being able to be a good mom to Jacob had also brought Sarah's observations regarding Anna to mind.

Eli let go of the steering wheel, flexing his fingers as he let out a long breath. He wished that he could exhale all the emotion he was dealing with. Life had become more complicated with Noah's birth, but it was a complication that they'd welcomed. All the stuff since then, however, was unexpected, and the smooth sailing he'd anticipated as they'd moved into parenthood hadn't manifested itself.

He loved Noah with all his heart, but him not being a good sleeper and fussy so much of the time was wearing on both him and Anna. And now he had Jacob to think about because he realized that they might need to take the teen in on a more permanent basis. After his conversation with Josie, it was clear that she couldn't take him, and neither could Pete. In Eli's mind, there was no one left to care for the boy but him.

After sitting for a few more minutes, mulling over the situation and the options, Eli spent some time praying about it all. This situation was so beyond him. It was more than he could handle on his own, and he prayed that God would give him wisdom and strength to carry the burdens that now rested on his shoulders.

When he got home a short time later, his mom was in the kitchen with Jacob, baking cookies. He was surprised, but her presence was a reminder that he wasn't alone. His mom had been his strength for so long, and he knew she would always be there for him.

"Hello, darling," his mom said as he approached them. Though she smiled at him, her gaze held concern. "We decided to make some cookies."

"What kind are you making?" he asked, directing his question to Jacob.

"Peanut butter chocolate chip."

"Oh, like *Reese's?*"

Jacob nodded. "I like peanut butter and chocolate. It's my favorite."

"They smell amazing. Have you tried one?"

"We're just waiting for them to cool a bit," Jacob said.

"I can't wait to try one." He looked back at his mom. "Where's Anna?"

"She went to put Noah down and try to sleep herself."

"I'm going to grab the monitor so she can keep sleeping if he wakes up."

"Sounds good. If you want to take a nap as well, go ahead. I'll listen for Noah."

It was tempting, but he needed to spend some time with Jacob. "I'll be okay. Anna needs to rest more than I do."

His mom didn't look convinced, but she nodded. Eli left the two of them and went to their bedroom. It was dark, and he moved quietly to Anna's side of the bed to grab the monitor.

"I'm awake," Anna said as he reached for it.

Leaving it where it was, he sat down on the bed beside her, resting his hand on her hip. "I'm going to take the monitor so you can rest."

"I don't know if I can fall asleep."

Her whispered words hit at his heart. "Why not, sweetheart?"

She sighed. "Too many things on my mind."

Eli understood that, and he hated that she was struggling in that way, too. If she could just fall asleep, it would help a lot, but he knew that wasn't how things worked for her.

He gently rubbed her back, praying that God would calm her mind and allow her to rest.

"I love you." He whispered the words, wishing they could make everything right, but he knew that his love couldn't fix everything.

"Love you too."

At least they still had that. He bent over and pressed a kiss to her cheek. "Sleep. We'll take care of Noah."

She gave a nod, then he picked up the monitor and left her to chase her ever-elusive sleep. They still had to talk about the appointment he needed to make for her the next day, but that could wait.

Back downstairs, he discovered that another batch of cookies had come out of the oven. He sat down at the kitchen table, and after checking that the monitor was on, he set it on the table.

"Do you like baking?" Eli asked.

"I've never baked before," Jacob said. "I would do some cooking, though, since... uh..." He stopped, his brow furrowed, and cleared his throat. "Since Mom didn't always want to cook."

Eli's heart hurt as his brain filled in the picture of Jacob trying to cook food for himself and Sheila. "What type of foods do you like?"

Jacob shrugged. "We ate a lot of mac and cheese and ramen."

"If you want anything specific, let me know, and we'll try to get it for you."

The teen nodded, but he kept his gaze on the cookies that were cooling on the rack in front of him. "Will I be able to talk to Bobby soon?"

Eli had totally forgotten about his friend. "Sure. As soon as you're done with the cookies, we can call his mom's cell. Will that be okay?"

"Yes. Thank you."

His mom helped Jacob spoon the last of the dough onto a cookie sheet which they transferred into the oven.

"Have you had a cookie yet?"

"Yeah. It was really good."

"Can I try one?"

Jacob looked up at Nadine, who nodded at him, then he picked a cookie off the cooling rack and brought it to Eli.

"Thank you." Eli took the cookie and bit into it, enjoying the combined flavors of peanut butter and chocolate. "This is delicious."

For a brief moment, a smile changed Jacob's face, and the grief relaxed its hold on his features.

"He did a great job," his mom said.

"What are you going to have him try next, Mom?"

"I don't know." She smiled at Jacob. "We'll talk about it and figure something out. There are so many possibilities."

His mom instructed Jacob through the kitchen cleanup, and Eli tried to relax. He closed his eyes, letting the conversation between his mom and Jacob flow around him.

This was not how he'd ever envisioned his life. But he, more than most, knew that life could take some really bizarre turns. Nothing should surprise him anymore.

Once the cookies were all done cooling and put away, Eli placed a call to Bobby's mom and managed to set up a video chat for the boys. He left Jacob chatting in the living room and joined his mom at the dining room table, where she sat with a cup of tea.

"He's a lovely boy," she said, keeping her voice low.

"He is," El agreed.

"What are you going to do?"

Eli sighed as he ran a hand over his face. "I don't know, Mom. I just don't know." He paused. "Did Sarah talk to you?"

His mom took a sip of her tea, looking at him over the rim of the cup. "Yes. She mentioned her concerns about Anna last night."

"Do you think she's right?"

His mom hesitated before nodding. "I'm not very familiar with postpartum depression, but as Sarah talked to me about it, I could see how it might be what Anna is struggling with."

"I don't know what to do."

"You focus on Anna," she said. "Sarah and I will be here to help with Jacob and Noah."

Eli glanced over to where Jacob was chatting with Bobby. "I haven't been able to talk to Anna about it, but I think we need to keep Jacob."

His mom's brows lifted briefly, then she said, "Pete or Josie can't take him?"

He shook his head. "Plus, he thinks I'm his dad. How can I hit him with another loss?"

"He would be fortunate to have you as his father," his mom said. "But yes, you need to speak to Anna about it. If she really is struggling with postpartum depression, she might find it challenging to have another child to care for."

Eli sighed, again feeling torn in two directions. Before he had a chance to say anything, the sound of fussing came over the monitor. He sat for a minute to see if Noah would settle again, but when he didn't, Eli got to his feet and headed for the stairs.

When he reached the room, he found that Anna had somehow beaten him there. As she lifted Noah from the crib, Eli said, "Let me take him, sweetheart."

"I couldn't sleep," she said as she carried Noah to the change table and laid him down.

For the first time, maybe because he was actually listening for it, Eli heard a note of despair in Anna's voice, and fear crept into his heart. Despair had led to Sheila taking her life, and he didn't want Anna to ever get to that point.

As she lifted Noah up, Eli wrapped his arms around them both, vowing to do what he had to in order to make sure that Anna got through whatever she was struggling with.

~*~

On Monday morning, Anna swung her legs over the side of the bed and sat up, abandoning her attempt to nap. Her shoulders slumped as she sat on the edge of the bed. Eli had insisted yet again that she try to sleep when Noah went down for his morning nap. But, as usual, her mind had just rocketed from one thing to another as she tried to cope with everything in her life. Everything including Jacob and what was going on with his situation.

As she walked down the stairs a few minutes later, Anna heard voices. She frowned when she recognized Sarah's. What was she doing there? Not that she didn't want the woman around. It was just that after weeks of only seeing her periodically at the lodge, she'd been at the house twice in three days.

"Hi, sweetheart," Eli said when she walked into the living room. He was sat on the floor with Noah propped up between his legs.

Jacob knelt in front of them, rolling a ball to Noah, then leaning over to retrieve and roll it to him again. Judging from Noah's squeals, it was a game he highly approved of.

Sarah was on the couch with her legs tucked up beside her. She smiled at Anna and gave a little wave.

"What's brought you by again so soon?" Anna asked, hoping she didn't sound rude. She seemed to have lost her ability to judge that anymore.

Sarah and Eli exchanged a look, then Eli said, "We have an appointment to go to, and Sarah is going to watch Noah and Jacob for us."

Anna frowned. "An appointment? With who? Did I forget something?"

If that was the case, it wouldn't surprise her at all.

"No, you didn't. I made the appointment this morning with the doctor," Eli said. " *Your* doctor."

"My doctor?" Anna crossed her arms. "Why?"

Eli gestured for Sarah with a wave, and she got up and switched places with him behind Noah. With a cautious look on his face, Eli approached Anna, then guided her to the kitchen.

"What's going on?" Anna asked, anger and confusion growing within her. "Why would you make an appointment with my doctor without talking with me?"

"I'm worried about you." The concern on Eli's face deepened. "You're not sleeping. You seem... unhappy."

"I'm not unhappy," Anna protested. But maybe that wasn't entirely the truth. "And as for not sleeping, I sleep when I can, but you know that Noah isn't sleeping well himself."

"Just humor me, sweetheart," Eli said, lifting a hand to her cheek. "I love you, and it hurts to see you struggling."

Anna didn't know what to say. Going to the doctor seemed to be admitting that something was wrong, and she really didn't think there was anything wrong beyond her just not getting enough sleep. A couple of nights of solid sleep and she'd be fine.

Probably. Hopefully. Maybe...?

Anna rubbed her mouth, but then pulled her hand away when she realized her fingers were trembling. She clenched her hand into a fist, not wanting anyone to see.

"We should take Noah with us," Anna said, reluctant to leave him, even for just an hour.

Eli cupped her face in his hands. "He'll be fine with Sarah, love. Mom will drop by as well. He's in very good hands."

It wasn't that Anna didn't trust Sarah. It was just that she should be the one looking after her baby. He was her responsibility. Her only responsibility these days since she couldn't seem to get motivated to do any work beyond posting the odd video or picture that made it seem like she was busy living her best life as a new mom.

"The sooner we go, the sooner we'll be back," Eli said.

Knowing that this was a battle she would not win, Anna nodded. "Just let me put on a little makeup."

Eli nodded and let her go, returning to the living room as she made her way back to the bedroom. Makeup wasn't something she'd worn a lot of in the past few months, but it didn't take her long to layer on concealer under her eyes, add some mascara to her lashes and some gloss to her lips.

When she got back, she found Jacob was still rolling the ball back and forth in front of Noah, and the baby didn't appear to have tired of the game yet.

Sarah looked up and smiled. "Don't you worry about Noah. He's going to be just fine with me. I love the little goober." She pressed a kiss to his head. "And he loves his favorite auntie. Don't you, buddy?"

"I have been showing him pictures of Leah, so he'll be happy to see her when she comes home," Eli said.

"So rude!" Sarah exclaimed. "I'm here, so I'm his favorite."

"We can take him with us," Anna said again.

"Nope. This is Auntie-Nephew time." Sarah shooed them with her hands. "Off you go."

"Thanks, sis," Eli said, placing his hand on Anna's back. "Let's go, love. The sooner we go, the sooner we'll be back."

Anna allowed Eli to guide her out the door and into their SUV. Worry ate at her as they drove away from the cabin. If something happened to Noah while they were gone, she could never live with herself.

"He'll be fine," Eli said, repeating himself for what he probably thought was the millionth time. But in true Eli fashion, there was no impatience or frustration in his voice.

"I know." But did she? She really didn't think there was any reason for her to go to the doctor on such short notice, so being away from him felt unnecessary.

There was no sense in arguing now that they'd left the house, though. All she could do was cooperate, so she could be back home sooner rather than later.

CHAPTER EIGHT

Jacob focused on the ball as he gently rolled it to the baby. The woman who sat behind Noah seemed nice. She was his aunt, he supposed, since she was his dad's sister.

It was weird to be left with yet another stranger, and Jacob was starting to wonder if his life was destined to be full of strangers. Would anyone take the time to get to know him? Would he even want that? Having lost his mom, he felt like the hole in his heart was so big, there was no room for anyone else.

And then there was Anna. He'd watched her over the past day, noticing how she seemed to zone out at times, staring blankly at nothing. It was a look he'd seen on his mom's face, and it scared him. Jacob didn't want Noah to endure what he had. And he didn't want to witness another woman lose her fight with the darkness inside her.

Jacob hoped Eli could get her the help that his mom had never gotten.

"So, Jacob, tell me about yourself."

He glanced up and saw the woman smiling at him, her expression friendly. "What do you want to know?"

"What do you like to do?"

"Play video games."

"That's a pretty normal activity for kids your age, huh?"

Jacob nodded. Hopefully, Eli would be able to get him a gaming console soon so that he could play games with his best friend.

"What games do you play?"

"Mainly Fortnite, but also some Minecraft."

"I'm afraid to say that I know nothing about video games. Unfortunately, I'm not sure if there are any of us in the family who really understand video games." She paused for a moment. "Although maybe Beau's brother or Gavin might know more about them."

"Gavin?"

"He's my twin sister's husband."

"You have a twin?"

"Yep. We're identical, but I'll share the secret of how to tell us apart."

"Okay?"

Sarah leaned forward a bit, her gaze holding a hint of laughter. "I'm the one that smiles."

Jacob stared at her. "Your sister doesn't smile?"

"Oh, she does," Sarah said as she sat back. "But I smile more. Leah is reserved, but she's nice. Though don't tell her I said that."

Jacob wasn't sure what to make of this woman. She was friendly and seemed to be interested in him. "Is she going to come here?"

"She's on her honeymoon at the moment, but she'll be home soon."

Jacob looked down at the ball and ran his fingers over the smooth surface. Part of him wanted to hate this woman for being so happy when his mom had struggled so much. Why couldn't his own mom have had the happy life this woman obviously had?

He glanced around the living room, taking in the comfortable furniture and the large fireplace, as well as the pictures of his dad and his family scattered around the room. If his mom and dad hadn't broken up, was this where he would have lived? Surely a home like this one would have been something his mom would have enjoyed. And if she'd been happy, he would still have her.

"Are you doing okay, Jacob?" Sarah asked softly. "I'm sure it hasn't been easy."

He didn't want to look at her for fear that the tears that suddenly stung his eyes might fall. "I'm okay."

"You don't have to be," she said. "You're in a place where you'll be supported as you grieve for your mom. No one will judge you for crying, and we'll be here if you need to talk."

Jacob glanced up at her for a moment before looking back down at the colorful ball. Noah squealed, demanding attention that Jacob was only too glad to give him. Anything was better than thinking about the aching hole in his heart.

"Do you have kids?" he asked, not wanting the focus on himself anymore.

"Not yet," she said. "But hopefully someday."

"Does your sister have kids?"

"Nope. She and Gavin just got married."

Jacob wished that his mom had gotten married, even if it hadn't been to his dad, because then he'd still have had someone after she died. And maybe she wouldn't have felt the need to escape life if they'd had a man like Eli to love and care for them.

Unfortunately, he knew that love wasn't enough to anchor someone if they were determined to float away. After all, the love he and his mom had shared hadn't been enough to make her want to stay with him.

Silence fell again, interrupted only by Noah's impatient squeals. Jacob had a lot of questions he wanted to ask Sarah about his dad, but he didn't voice them. He worried that asking more questions would open the door to her asking questions of him, which he didn't want.

He was in a tough place. Part of him wanted to talk about his mom and share about their lives together because he was afraid that if he didn't talk about her, he was going to forget her. But another part didn't want to remember the hard life they'd shared.

Most of all, though, he didn't want to break down crying in front of this friendly woman.

"I guess you'll be going to school," Sarah said. "What grade are you in?"

"Grade seven." His stomach clenched at the idea of a new school.

"Do you like school?"

"Not really." He didn't have a problem with the work, but he hated the way the kids picked on him because he was smaller than most of the other boys in his grade, and even some of the girls.

"I didn't like schoolwork much," Sarah said. "But I liked hanging out with my friends."

"My friend is back in Shreveport."

"You'll make new friends."

Jacob didn't want new friends. He wanted Bobby. "Maybe I can do school online."

Sarah gave a soft hum. "I'm not sure how that works."

Jacob didn't either, but it was an option that appealed to him more than going to a new school. He hoped his dad would be willing to consider it. He would work hard and not be any trouble at home, and he'd help with Noah, too. Anything so he wouldn't have to go to a new school.

But somehow, he doubted that what he wanted was going to be taken into consideration. After all, if it had been, he'd still be in Shreveport, living with Bobby and Lynn.

"Is Anna okay?" he asked, once again wanting to move away from a subject that caused his stomach to hurt. Everything in his life seemed to be a subject he wanted to avoid talking about.

When Sarah didn't answer right away, Jacob glanced up at her. She was frowning, an expression that seemed out of place on her face. With a sigh, she brushed her hand over Noah's head.

"Sometimes, after a woman has a baby, her hormones and other things can make her... struggle a bit."

Jacob nodded. "Depression?"

"Yes. It's possible she's struggling with postpartum depression."

His stomach twisted at the thought. But maybe she'd be okay because she had people around her who cared and would get her help.

"But Eli is going to help her. You don't have to worry about Anna."

"Sure."

"How about we get something to eat?" Sarah said as she got to her feet, then scooped Noah up. "Are you hungry?"

He wasn't, but maybe she needed something else to focus on. "I could maybe eat."

"Well, let's see what there is. Noah, bubby, you're going to have to settle for mashed bananas or something."

Jacob abandoned the ball and followed her into the kitchen. He climbed up on a stool at the counter while she put Noah in a chair thing that sat on the counter next to him.

"Want a sandwich?" she asked. "Or would you prefer soup?"

"A sandwich is fine."

Sarah seemed familiar with the kitchen as she began to pull out stuff and put it on the counter. "Ham or turkey?"

"Ham."

"You want cheese? Tomatoes?"

"Cheese, please." He wrinkled his nose. "No tomatoes."

"Not a fan?" Sarah asked with a laugh.

"Not at all."

"So you don't like spaghetti?"

"I do, just not with chunks of tomatoes. "

"Okay. No tomatoes. Mayo? Mustard?"

Sarah worked quickly as she spoke, laying out bread and plopping slices of deli ham and cheese on them.

"I like mustard, but no mayo." He really wasn't that hungry, but he still took the plate she slid across the counter to him. "Thank you."

"You're welcome."

As he ate small bites of the sandwich, he watched as Sarah made another sandwich, this time putting on everything he'd left off. She also mashed up a banana in a small bowl and, between bites of her sandwich, she fed Noah spoonfuls. The baby seemed to spit most of the banana back out and then smeared it over his hands and face.

When he said as much, Sarah laughed. "Yeah. Thankfully, he doesn't really need the food to survive. He still gets most of his nutrition from formula, but he needs to learn to eat solid food."

Watching Noah made Jacob want to smile, but grief made it hard. He wasn't sure how he was supposed to grieve his mom's death. Grief had always been something that happened to other people, and grieving seemed like what you did to get over a person dying.

He would never get over his mom's death. He just knew it. So was he going to be grieving for the rest of his life? Always one comment, one memory, away from tears? His chest ached at the thought. He set his sandwich down, and his hand went to cover his heart.

Would his life just be made up of small blips of happiness? His mom hadn't seemed to even have that much, so maybe he shouldn't hope for that for himself. Grief would be what stayed with him, along with his mom's memory.

He couldn't let himself forget her.

~*~

Anna glanced over at Eli, hating that she'd let him down. As the doctor had asked her questions, she'd realized that she had to be honest this time. Unlike previous times when she'd kind of fudged her responses a bit.

Being honest was hard, though. Baring her soul felt like admitting that she couldn't do what every other woman could. That she wasn't capable of handling her roles of wife and mother.

"Anna." The doctor's voice was firm, yet gentle. "I need you to listen to me. I'm sure you've got a voice in your head telling you differently, but you need to know that you haven't done anything wrong. You're doing a great job with Noah. From what you've said, he's healthy and thriving."

Anna frowned. "But he seems so fussy and unhappy most of the time."

"That's not because you've done something wrong."

"He's still not sleeping through the night."

"But that doesn't necessarily mean there's something wrong," the doctor said. "There are some children who just don't need as much sleep. You're focusing on the stories you've heard about babies who sleep through the night and take long naps. The reality is that while there are babies who do sleep like that, there are also babies like Noah who don't. It doesn't mean you've done anything wrong, and it doesn't mean anything is wrong with Noah."

Anna listened to his words, but she struggled to take them to heart. Hearing that some babies were just fussier or didn't sleep as well as others didn't matter when she was worried about *her* baby.

"But let's talk about you specifically," the doctor said. "From our conversation here today, I do believe that you're dealing with postpartum depression. Now, there are antidepressants that can help."

Anna shook her head before he even finished his sentence.

"You wouldn't have to be on them indefinitely," he said. "However, if you don't want to go that route, there are other things you can try."

"Like what?"

"I want you to speak with someone who specializes in postpartum depression. Also, I want you to be mindful in taking care of yourself, not just Noah." The doctor glanced at Eli before focusing on her again. "Take time to exercise. Get outside for some fresh air. Make sure you're eating regularly, and that it's healthy food.

But here's the big one, and the one you'll probably struggle with. *Accept help.* If you didn't get enough sleep the night before, let Grandma watch the baby so you can nap. And Dad, that goes for you too. It's not a failure to ask for help, and it's not a failure for you to accept help when it's offered."

Anna glanced at Eli before looking down at her clenched hands. She knew that was her biggest struggle: equating accepting help with failing. But that was how she'd been raised. Her parents had set an example of self-sufficiency and had expected the same of her.

As an adult, she'd struck out on her own, pursuing a career as a content creator and influencer. Her parents had supported her but also expected her to take care of herself and not expect people to do things for her.

Her mom would likely be disappointed that she hadn't been able to handle all this on her own. She should have been able to.

"Do you think you can do that?"

"We'll work on it," Eli said when Anna hesitated. "Both of us together."

"Excellent. Support is very important when dealing with post-partum depression. Let your husband help you. Let your family help you."

Ana let out a sigh. "I'll try."

After consulting his computer, the doctor scribbled something on a pad of paper on his desk, then ripped off the top sheet. When he held it out, Eli took it from him.

"That's the therapist's information. Give her a call."

"We will."

"Also, make an appointment to come back and see me next week," the doctor said with a stern look at the two of them. "I'll want to hear what steps you've taken throughout the week. I want to make sure that we're headed in the right direction."

Eli nodded and stood up. Anna was slower getting to her feet, feeling the weight of expectation that she get *this* right now, in addition to everything else. She left the room with Eli and stood quietly at his side as he made the appointment for the following week.

As they left the doctor's office, Eli took her hand. Anna clung to him, desperate for the strength he offered.

Once they were back in the SUV, Anna said, "I'm sorry."

"No," Eli replied. "You have nothing to apologize for. If anyone should apologize, it should be *me*. I didn't realize what was happening."

"That's because I didn't tell you how I've been feeling."

"That stops now," Eli said, shifting in his seat to face her more fully. "We're in this together, love. That's what our vows meant to me. You're not alone. Noah is our son, so we need to support each other as we raise him. Through the good and the not-so-good."

Anna nodded, trying to ignore how her eyes stung with unshed tears. She hoped that she could do what was necessary. It sounded so easy—accept help—but for her, that was going to be a challenge.

"Let's get something to eat before we head home," Eli suggested. "Sarah said she had no problem feeding the boys."

The *boys*. Plural. For the duration of the appointment, she'd forgotten that there was another child in their lives now. That was a discussion they still needed to have.

During their meal, however, she didn't bring it up, and neither did Eli. Instead, they talked about less weighty things, like the projects Eli was working on. Though she knew that they absolutely needed to talk about Jacob, she was glad for the brief break from discussing his situation.

Their time together felt like a date, and she cherished it. She couldn't remember the last time it had just been the two of them out for a meal. Even before Noah was born, they hadn't gone out much since her ability to eat had been curtailed by the nausea she had struggled with.

"I know we have other things we need to talk about," Eli said as they walked back to the SUV once they'd finished their meal. "We might not be able to cover everything in one sitting, but we will discuss it all, I promise."

Anna knew that Eli would keep his word, and she would have to do her part and be honest about how she was feeling. She'd kind of done that already in the doctor's office, but they hadn't talked about Jacob yet. Somehow, she had to gather her thoughts about that situation before they did.

CHAPTER NINE

Sarah was impressed that Jacob did as she asked, loading their dishes into the dishwasher without complaint. For some reason, she'd figured that a teenage boy wouldn't help without showing some attitude. Her mom had shared that Jacob seemed to enjoy baking with her the previous afternoon, so Sarah was happy to see that his helpful attitude hadn't been a fluke.

He'd also proven to be helpful with Noah, distracting him while Sarah finished putting away the last of the food she'd used to make them lunch, and then prepared a bottle for Noah. It would make things a lot easier for Eli and Anna if Jacob was an easygoing kid.

It had been an interesting few days—even without Jacob's arrival in their lives. Though clearly the news about Sheila and Jacob had been what had brought her into closer contact with Anna. Until she'd spent the night there, Sarah had just assumed the tiredness she'd witnessed whenever the family had been together was just normal for a mom of a young baby.

She'd thought maybe she was just imagining things. But when Beau had mentioned how zoned out and down Anna seemed to be, she'd paid more attention to her. It hurt Sarah's heart that she hadn't seen it sooner, because clearly her sister-in-law had been struggling.

"Do you want to give Noah his bottle?" Sarah asked as she walked to the Exersaucer, where she'd put Noah after lunch.

"I can do that?" Jacob frowned. "I don't want to hurt him."

"I'll help you," Sarah assured him. "It'll be fine."

She lifted Noah from the seat, then had Jacob sit next to her on the couch. Noah was squirming around a bit, but once she handed over the bottle, he grabbed onto it with both hands and settled right down.

Jacob held him tightly, but Sarah didn't move away from them since the teen probably hadn't dealt with babies much, if at all. She wasn't sure if Anna would be happy that she was letting Jacob help, but she felt a strong need to try and give the boy some positive experiences.

"I can't believe that I was this small once."

Sarah wondered how much he knew about his baby years, but she didn't ask. "We all started out about the same size. Leah and I were a little smaller than normal to start with since we were born a bit earlier than we should have been."

"Mama said I was a small baby too, but my friend's mom said he was a chunky baby." Jacob sighed. "I'm still small."

"You just haven't hit your growth spurt yet," Sarah tried to assure him.

"Was my... dad ever small like me?"

Sarah cringed inwardly. "I don't really remember, to be honest. But even if he wasn't, that doesn't mean there's anything wrong with the way you are. We all grow at different rates."

Noah made quick work of his bottle, then proceeded to fling it onto the floor. Sarah reached over and took him from Jacob while Jacob rescued the bottle.

The baby was probably due for a nap, but she wasn't sure about putting him down. Eli and Anna might prefer to have him sleep when they got home so that Anna could nap at the same time.

Sarah put Noah back in the Exersaucer, then went to the kitchen to rinse out the bottle. She loved her nephew dearly, but she had to admit that even though she'd been thinking of having kids sooner rather than later, Noah had her reconsidering that plan.

She kept some pretty wacky hours with her painting, and she also loved sleep. And while Noah also seemed to keep wacky hours, he *didn't* love to sleep. Maybe it was time to have a conversation with Beau about it all.

When Anna and Eli arrived home a short time later, Sarah was sad to see that her sister-in-law looked even more stressed out. It had probably been expecting too much to hope she'd come home happier after a single appointment with her doctor.

"I'll go put Noah down," Anna said as she lifted him up. "And then I'm going to try to sleep too."

Sarah watched them go, then looked over at Jacob. The boy's brow was furrowed, and she wished that she could read his mind. Overall, that skill would come in handy in dealing with the boy's mental health needs. Unfortunately, she *still* didn't have that ability.

"I hope she'll be okay," he said, his voice soft.

"I think she will be." Sarah wished that had been the case for his mom. But there was nothing they could do for Sheila now except take care of her son.

When Eli came back down, he handed the tablet he carried to Jacob. "You can play on that for a while, if you'd like. I suppose Bobby is still at school?"

Jacob nodded. "We usually didn't get home until around four." He lifted the tablet. "I'll just play on this."

He settled into the corner of the couch, drawing his knees up as he bent over the tablet. Sarah followed Eli into the kitchen, where he went straight to the coffeemaker. She settled on a stool at the island counter, watching as he made a cup of coffee.

"You want one?" he asked once his cup was ready.

"No, I'm good."

Eli leaned against the counter opposite her. "Well, we have a plan of action, I think."

"That's good."

"Yeah. I was sure that she would deny that anything was wrong. Good thing the doctor has previous experience with postpartum."

"So, what can we do to help?"

"The doctor has instructed us to ask for help and to accept it when it's offered, among other things. Also, he wants her to see a therapist who specializes in this. He suggested medication, but she said no."

"I'm glad that things seem to be moving in the right direction. We'll certainly be praying for both of you, and you can count on us for anything. If we haven't offered and you need help, please ask. You know Mom, Beau, and I will do whatever we can."

"I know. I feel like I've been running a bit blind with all of us, to the detriment of Anna." Eli took a sip of his coffee, then sighed.

Sarah saw a weariness in her brother that hadn't been there in years. It was terribly hard to see it again. This time, however, she had confidence in Eli, knowing that his maturity and willingness to turn to God for wisdom and strength would help him navigate everything currently going on.

"I feel like I've failed her," Eli murmured, his gaze going to where Anna had disappeared up the stairs with Noah. "But I know that she also feels like she failed me and Noah. Somehow, we just need to let those feelings go and move forward."

"I think the important thing is that Noah is healthy, and he is. Now we just need to get Anna to that point."

"You know, when we talked about becoming parents, we didn't think it would be a walk in the park. However, we didn't realize how very difficult it could be. It was like Noah read all the parenting books before we did and decided he was going to do the opposite of what was expected. I mean, when they mention sleeping like a baby, I didn't think it meant catnaps and up and down all night long."

"I've decided that perhaps I'm not ready to give up my sleep just yet."

Eli gave a huff of laughter. "Yeah. It really is something to consider."

"Well, now that Noah is weaned, Beau and I can stay overnight here if you and Anna want to sleep at the lodge or one of the cabins."

"She might be willing to do that, especially since we'd still be close if Noah needed us."

By the time Sarah left, she and Eli had come up with a few ways that she and their mom could help them. They hadn't discussed Jacob, but it wasn't as if they could do that when he was sitting within earshot.

Sarah wouldn't be surprised if Jacob's arrival had added to the stress Anna was feeling, but she didn't know what they could do to help with that. It wouldn't be fair to take him to their home when what he needed right then was stability. He didn't need to be passed around.

Since it wasn't possible for Jacob's grandfather or aunt to take him, what did it mean for the teen? Would Eli take him in permanently? Even though he wasn't his biological father?

Sarah was glad it wasn't a decision she was responsible for making. About all they could do was pray for Anna and Eli as they sorted it out. She just hoped that whatever happened, Jacob wouldn't experience even more hurt than he already had.

~*~

"We need to talk about Jacob," Anna said.

Eli looked up from his phone to see Anna coming out of their bathroom. It wasn't that late, but since both Jacob and Noah were in bed, they'd decided to call it a day as well. He wished that they could just go to sleep, but Anna was right. The only problem was that he didn't have an answer to the question she was going to ask.

She came to the bed and slid under the covers. Letting out a sigh, she relaxed back against her pile of pillows, then looked over at him. "What's happening with Jacob?"

"I don't know."

"I thought you were just picking him up and then you'd hand him over to his family."

Then it was Eli's turn to sigh. "I don't think that is going to happen."

Anna frowned. "I don't understand."

"Pete just moved into a small apartment, and he doesn't have room for Jacob. Josie is a live-in nurse, and I'm not sure she'll be able to take Jacob in."

"So, what are you going to do with him?"

Eli wished so much that Jacob had come into their lives at a different time. Perhaps before Noah, or after they'd worked through Anna's postpartum depression. There was no way that Anna was going to be able to look at the situation with Jacob objectively. And he didn't blame her for that.

She was already struggling, and Jacob had come to them with his own set of complications. Eli didn't know how to help them both. It was clear that if he gave one what they needed, it would be at the expense of the other. What was he supposed to do?

"What do *you* want me to do?" Eli asked. Maybe that would give him a place to start.

"Don't push this off on me," Anna said with a rare flash of anger. "If he really isn't your son, then he's also not your responsibility."

"What do you mean, *if?*" Eli asked, his stomach clenching. "I told you that I wasn't involved physically with Sheila. He *can't* be mine."

"Then why didn't she contact his actual father instead of you?"

He hadn't told her the details about Jacob's conception yet, but he shouldn't have needed to. She should have accepted his word. It felt like the trust he'd always assumed they had between them was just... gone.

No. It wasn't gone. He had to remember that Anna was struggling. Her reactions to things weren't what her usual reactions would be. He didn't have that same excuse, so he needed to keep a calm head.

It was just so hard because he hated that she was suffering, and he also missed the Anna she'd been before these past few months. It hadn't changed his love for her. He didn't think anything could. This was just a rough patch that they would get through as long as they persevered.

"Sheila was raped," Eli said. "She never knew who his biological father was."

Anna frowned. "She was raped?"

"Yes. It happened not long after she left here, which is why Jacob's age fits a timeline for him to be mine. But he's not."

"You want him to be, though."

Eli didn't know how to answer that. It wasn't that he wished that he was Jacob's biological father. It was more that Jacob needed someone, and Eli wasn't sure who else could be there for him the way he could.

"Love, I don't know what to do. My heart tells me that Jacob is ours."

"How could you know that already? You haven't even known him for a week."

Eli wasn't sure how to explain it. He honestly didn't understand it himself. It made no sense for Sheila to list him—of all people—as Eli's father. But since she had, it seemed more complicated to reject the role than to accept it. Especially because it was likely that for his whole life, Jacob had thought a man named Eli McNamara was his father.

"I feel like God has arranged all of this."

"Or maybe you were supposed to just be the conduit to get Jacob to his actual family."

"And devastate a boy who has just lost his mom by rejecting him?"

Anna rubbed her face. "I don't know either. It just doesn't feel like we're his family."

"We do need to make a decision soon, I think. I can't register him for school as his father, only to then say, *Oh, I'm not really his dad* and turn him over to someone else. That's not fair to Jacob. He's so young to be experiencing all of this. I think I just want to offer him some stability."

Anna sat forward with slumped shoulders, staring down at her hands. She sighed, then slid down further under the covers, turning on her side to face away from him. "We'd better get some sleep. Noah will probably wake up soon."

"Love..." Eli couldn't imagine going to sleep with things so unsettled between them.

"Not tonight. I just... I can't think anymore."

He understood that feeling because his brain and heart hurt from being pulled in different directions. Reaching out, he snapped off the lamp on his side of the bed, then checked to make sure the monitor was turned up enough before he laid down.

After a brief hesitation, he moved closer to Anna. He rested his hand on her hip, even though normally he would have curled up around her. He wanted to be sensitive to her moods, but he also didn't want her to think that he was angry with her.

Her hand settled over his, threading her fingers through his, then she pulled his hand forward to rest against her waist. Relief spiraled through Eli as he shifted closer to her. The unsettledness they were facing might strain things, but it wouldn't break them. He wouldn't let it.

"I love you," he whispered.

"Love you too."

As long as they could keep that focus, everything would be okay.

CHAPTER TEN

Anna watched as Eli left with Jacob. They were on their way to visit Josie. She wasn't sure what she expected from the visit. Selfishly, she hoped that after meeting Jacob, Josie would want to have him live with her. But after the conversation she and Eli had had the night before, she didn't think that was likely to happen.

Once the SUV had disappeared from sight, Anna stared at the trees surrounding the house. The shade trees had all lost their leaves, while the evergreens were a reminder that this upcoming weekend was when she would usually decorate for Christmas. But she wasn't in the mood to do it. Nor was she in the mood to celebrate Thanksgiving.

Thankfully, Nadine and Leah were shouldering the bulk of the Thanksgiving meal. They had tasked her with bringing a salad. Usually, that would be what Sarah was assigned to bring, which told Anna just how little they felt they could depend on her these days.

But she wasn't going to ask for more responsibility. That would just be stupid, given how she currently felt.

She needed to at least make an effort for Christmas, though. This was Noah's first Christmas, and she owed it to him to make it special, even if he wouldn't remember it. She also needed to seriously focus on getting some presents.

It seemed likely that she should add Jacob to her gift list. Not that she actually had a list.

Maybe she needed to focus on making that list. She'd let so much of how she usually lived her life slide during the last months of her pregnancy, and she'd never picked it back up. It had been ages since she'd last truly felt like herself.

Her reactions to situations were the clearest indicator that she wasn't herself. She was very fortunate that Eli was a man with tremendous patience and understanding.

Noah began to fuss in his highchair, where he'd been playing with the attachments on his tray. She went over and lifted him up. Setting him on her hip, she carried him back into the living room. She went to the roll-top desk that Eli had made for her and opened it for the first time in months.

The planner she'd purchased earlier that year sat where she'd left it eight months ago. She picked it up along with her favorite brand of blue gel pen. Though she could have used her phone for everything she put in the planner, she enjoyed writing stuff out.

Carrying both items over to the coffee table, she set Noah down in his curved pillow that gave him support for sitting. He was getting better at keeping his balance, but occasionally he tipped over, which would upset him. She set his favorite toys in front of him, then sat down beside him.

Once he seemed content with the setup, Anna turned her attention to her planner. She paused for a moment before flipping it open, feeling a bit afraid to read what her last notes might have been. Though she didn't keep a journal, per se, she had made a habit of jotting down a line or two each day about how she was feeling.

After paging back, she found her last entry, which had been in February as she'd started her seventh month of pregnancy. *I can't wait to have this little guy. The pain in my crotch and the never-ending nausea are wearing on me. I'm tired but can't sleep because I can't get comfortable, and everything hurts.*

She could acknowledge now that she was already sliding into a depressed state of mind at that point. Her mom and Nadine had talked about how easy their first—and in her mom's case, only—pregnancy had been, and Anna had just assumed that once she got past the first trimester, she would feel better.

When it became apparent that wasn't going to happen, she'd started keeping her struggles to herself. She'd wanted to breeze through her pregnancy like so many women seemed to. She'd planned for a maternity photo shoot and a video of pregnancy styles along with a nursery reveal. But she just hadn't felt up to producing any of them, and then she'd gone into labor weeks earlier than expected.

The long labor and delivery, followed by a rough recovery and a struggle to breastfeed had caused her to spiral down even further. Absolutely nothing had gone as she'd hoped, and the notes she'd made reflected that. It should really have come as no surprise that she'd ended up struggling with postpartum depression.

But she knew that for her sake—as well as Noah and Eli's—she needed to do what was necessary to get a handle on her life. Even though she had wanted to deny that anything was wrong, she obviously wasn't hiding her struggles as well as she'd hoped. She would try her best to do what the doctor had suggested, she'd go to the therapist, and if necessary, she'd even go on medication.

Eli had said that they'd go for a walk when he and Jacob got back if it wasn't raining, then they were going to the lodge for dinner since Gavin and Leah were supposed to return from their honeymoon that afternoon. At least she'd be getting some exercise.

For the next little while, she split her attention between Noah and her planner, making a list of gift ideas and also of activities that she could do each day to help bring some stability to her life. She wanted to be able to tell the doctor what she'd done, so he would know she was serious about working toward healing herself.

After a moment's hesitation, she penned in something she had been ignoring for so many reasons. Once Noah had been born, her daily devotions had ground to a halt. Even before he'd been born, they'd been sporadic. And it hadn't all been because she was tired or busy. Whether it made sense or not, she'd been struggling with anger toward God because of how things had gone over the past several months.

When Eli returned with Jacob, he brought home food from *Norma's*. She hadn't even thought about lunch, which was yet another reflection of her state of mind.

"How was the visit?" Anna asked as they unpacked the food at the dining room table.

Eli settled Noah in the crook of his arm as he sat down in his chair. "It went well."

"She lives in a mansion," Jacob said, his eyes going wide. "Like it's a huge house."

Anna had never seen the place, but she knew that Josie's employer was a wealthy philanthropist.

"And one of the guys she works for used to be a sniper." Jacob was showing signs of excitement that had been missing since he'd arrived.

"Kenneth's grandson was injured overseas and has retired from the military," Eli explained.

"So Josie is working as a live-in nurse for them both?"

"I think so. I didn't ask, to be honest." Noah waved his hands when Eli lifted his burger to take a bite. "Sorry, bud, you're not quite at the burger eating age yet."

Jacob had some chicken strips and fries, but he wasn't inhaling it like Anna had heard teenage boys did with their food. Anna watched him as she ate her chicken wrap, wondering if anyone would really accept that he was Eli's son. He looked completely different from Eli. Literally night and day.

Anna didn't participate much in the conversation, focusing on eating her meal, then taking Noah from Eli so he could finish his burger without the baby trying to grab it from him. She could have put him in his highchair, but she suspected he would loudly object to that.

"Ready to go for a walk?" Eli asked once the meal was done and cleared away.

She wasn't sure she was, but she didn't have a good excuse not to. "Let me go get my shoes and jacket."

When she got back, Eli had Noah bundled up and in his stroller. Jacob was talking with him as they waited on the front porch. Once Anna joined them, Eli maneuvered the stroller down the steps to the asphalt road that ran from their house all the way down to the lodge.

Maybe in the future, they'd go up the trail behind the house, but since the weather wasn't great, that wasn't a good plan with a baby. If it started to rain on this walk, at least they could duck into one of the empty cabins along the road.

"It's so quiet out here," Jacob said as they walked, his hands shoved into the front pocket of the hoodie that dwarfed his slim frame.

"Has it been hard for you to fall asleep without the noise of the city?" Eli asked. "Some of the guests we have out here have mentioned that."

"I don't know if it's that," Jacob said.

"Have you been sleeping okay?"

Anna realized as Eli asked the question that Jacob probably had a hard time falling asleep, and it likely had nothing to do with the lack of noise. She imagined that lying in bed at night was a horrible time for someone grieving the way Jacob was.

"I guess." There wasn't a lot of conviction in his voice.

Even though she wasn't super close with her parents, she couldn't imagine how difficult it would be to lose one of them. And to lose one to suicide? That would be even worse. She knew that people who committed suicide were likely listening to voices that were telling them untruths about themselves and their situation. But if one of her parents had died by suicide, she'd have had a hard time not thinking that they'd *chosen* to leave her. That they hadn't loved her enough to stay.

If she, as an adult, felt that way, she could only imagine that a child would feel the same way. Her gaze went to Jacob as he kept pace on the other side of Eli. She wished that she was in a better place emotionally to help him, but she felt like she was barely keeping her head above water as it was. It seemed unrealistic of Eli to expect her to take on the care of someone who needed emotional support the way Jacob did.

If she struggled just meeting Noah's needs, how could she hope to meet Jacob's?

"So you own all these?" Jacob asked, gesturing to the cabin they were passing.

"Our family does. Anna, my mom, and Leah—when she's here—take care of running things. My responsibility is to keep the buildings in good repair."

"Did you live here when my mom was here?"

"Yep. I've lived here my whole life. And my mom lived here when she was a girl too. This land has been in our family a long time."

"It's really nice around here," Jacob said. "Why would my mom leave?"

Anna glanced over at Eli and caught his gaze for a moment. She knew that Eli had hoped that his past with Sheila was well and truly behind him once Josie had found the letter which clarified that Sheila had left of her own accord. Unfortunately, Jacob's arrival in their lives made it impossible for them to ignore the past.

"She didn't like the small town," Eli said. "Plus, she had a... difficult relationship with her mom and wanted to get away from her."

"And you didn't go with her." It wasn't a question so much as a statement of fact, since clearly, Eli hadn't left when Sheila had.

"No. I couldn't go with her. My dad had left us, divorcing my mom, so she needed me to stay and help her and the twins."

"Did you know she was pregnant with me when she left?"

Anna exchanged glances with Eli again. She was pretty sure that he hadn't anticipated having this conversation on their little walk.

"No. I didn't. She left unexpectedly, not letting any of her friends or family know."

Jacob's head bent forward as he walked. "She should have stayed here. Maybe she wouldn't have died."

Anna understood why he would feel that way, but selfishly, she wasn't sure she would have wanted Sheila to hang around. If she had, would Sheila and Eli have continued their relationship? Or would things have still worked out the way they had for her and Eli?

"It's possible," Eli said.

Of course, if she hadn't left, Jacob wouldn't be alive. But mentioning that would reveal what Eli wasn't prepared to tell him yet.

Jacob continued to walk with hunched shoulders, and Anna felt her heart go out to him as he likely mulled over the *what if's* in his life. She could understand why his thoughts would go in that direction, but she knew from experience that it was a fruitless thought process. However, since she still struggled with imagining how things might be different, even knowing that was fruitless thinking, she doubted that Jacob could get a handle on it either.

Eli gestured for her to take over stroller duty, then stepped closer to Jacob. He rested his arm across the teen's shoulders.

"I know you miss your mom terribly," Eli said, his voice gentle. "When a parent leaves your life, it creates a big gaping hole. My dad didn't die, but he chose to not continue to be in our lives after he left. It was terrible for me, Leah, and Sarah. So I understand how hurtful it is to feel like a parent that you thought loved you decided to leave you."

Jacob looked up at Eli. "So, you don't see your dad?"

"No. He tried to step back into our lives a little while ago with his new family, but his motivations seemed... suspect to Sarah and Leah."

"But not to you?"

"He didn't try to talk to me. He seemed more interested in Sarah and Leah, so I let them make that call. If he'd attempted to talk to me, I might have felt differently."

"That sucks."

"Yes. It really does," Eli agreed. "I spent a lot of years being angry about him leaving... and other things. It really affected my life, and not in a good way."

"So you're telling me to not be angry about what's happened?"

"I'm telling you to not let anger take over your life. Be angry. Grieve. But don't let those emotions warp everything inside you."

"It's just not fair."

Anna was glad that Eli didn't come back with the pat response of *life isn't fair*. Her parents had used that phrase occasionally, and while it had been frustrating, it had also helped her to have a better perspective on how things worked in life. However, Jacob didn't need that particular perspective right then.

As they meandered closer to the lodge, Anna realized that she was getting a glimpse of the type of father Eli would be with Noah as a teen. It felt wrong of her to want to rob Jacob of that type of interaction. But would Eli be so distracted with Jacob that Noah would miss out?

Anna was very confused. She'd never felt like she was a super selfish person, but lately, it seemed as if focusing on her and Noah's needs made her selfish. She didn't know what to do about that.

Even though she had friends, Anna wasn't sure who to talk to about what was going on. Everyone was busy with their own lives. Jillian was adjusting to married life with her husband of seven months. Cara had given birth to her own baby not long ago.

Between feeling like a failure and not having her support group readily available, she'd been left adrift. But perhaps it was time that she swallowed her pride and reached out to let her friends know that she was struggling.

"Should we stop in and see Grandma, Noah?" Eli asked, bending forward to peer inside the stroller.

Noah had been surprisingly quiet throughout the walk. Apparently, being in the outdoors agreed with him. Their regular hikes had been something that had gone by the wayside with the difficulty of Anna's pregnancy, and they'd never picked it back up again after he'd been born.

As they reached the steps to the lodge, Eli took control of the stroller and got it up the stairs. When they walked in, Nadine greeted them all with smiles and hugs, then ushered them into the kitchen for a snack.

Nadine took Noah, and as she held him, she chatted with Jacob. Eli took care of making them some coffee, then settled down at the island beside Anna.

"Doing okay?" he asked.

She hated the worry on his face. Until she'd gotten pregnant, things had been so great. They'd had a partnership in the truest sense. She had her career. He had his. They worked together at the lodge when needed. The life they'd been building had filled her with contentment and anticipation. Adding a child to that life had been exactly what they wanted.

Unfortunately, they—or maybe it had just been her—had gone into the pregnancy with rose-colored glasses. But even then, when things had been rougher than she'd thought they'd be, there had been an end date to the pregnancy. There wasn't, however, an end date to the sleepless days and nights they were enduring with Noah.

In her current mindset, it was entirely likely that Noah was going to be an only child. But then she looked at where Jacob stood with Nadine and Noah, doing his best to make her baby smile. Or maybe, whether or not she wanted it, there already was another child in their lives.

CHAPTER ELEVEN

Jacob pulled his sweatshirt sleeves down over his hands, fisting his fingers in the fabric as he sat on the couch with Noah in his bouncy seat in front of him. His dad and Anna were getting stuff ready to go to the big lodge for Thanksgiving dinner.

Last year, Bobby's mom had invited them for Thanksgiving dinner. They hadn't had a turkey. Bobby's mom had bought a rotisserie chicken, and they'd had some mashed potatoes, stuffing, some carrots, and a small pumpkin pie for dessert. Somehow, he doubted that would be the case that day.

"Hey, Jacob," Eli called from the kitchen. "Come and give me a hand, please."

Noah gave a squeal of protest as Jacob walked to where Eli waited.

"Can you take this out to the SUV? Just pop the hatch and put it in the back."

Jacob took the diaper bag from him and headed out the front door. It was sort of raining, which was probably why they were going to take the SUV instead of walking the short distance.

He'd enjoyed the walk they'd taken, even though it had made him kind of sad. He really didn't understand why his mom had left New Hope Falls and his dad behind. Even though he hadn't seen much of the town, it seemed nicer than where they'd lived in Shreveport. He thought it might have been fun to grow up there, especially with his dad and grandparents close by.

When he went back inside, Anna was bundling Noah up. His dad picked up a zippered bag from the kitchen, then took it out to the car. Jacob hung around the door, waiting for Anna to finish with Noah. He could still see the strain on the woman's tired face, and he was pretty sure he was part of the reason for her stress.

No doubt, having the son her husband had fathered with a former girlfriend show up unexpectedly, hadn't helped her situation, but he knew he was the sole reason she seemed stressed out. Part of him wanted to tell her how lucky she was. She had a nice house and an extended family who supported her. Two things his mom hadn't had.

When she had Noah ready, she headed for the door. Eli came back in and waited for them both to leave the house before he closed and locked the door behind them.

Jacob was a bit nervous about the afternoon. Apparently, the unsmiling twin and her husband would be there, and from the conversation he'd heard, there would be some other people he hadn't met yet. Hopefully, they'd all be nice.

He climbed into the back of the SUV next to Noah's seat, then watched out the window as his dad drove them down the hill to the lodge. There were several cars parked there already, and he took a quick breath to try to calm his nerves. Unfortunately, it didn't really work.

Once parked, Anna went right in with Noah while his dad opened the back hatch. Jacob took the diaper bag again, slinging the strap over his shoulder, then followed his dad up the stairs and into the lodge.

The smell of food and the drone of conversation and bits of laughter greeted him as they walked in. It was a warm and welcoming environment, reminding him of the shows he and his mom had watched where there was a family who gathered together regularly, often with their friends. She'd told him that there really were families like that in real life, and he had to wonder if she'd been talking about this family.

"Here, I can take that," Anna said, holding out her hand.

Someone else must have taken the baby, since her arms were empty. He gave her the diaper bag, then moved off to the side, out of the way of everyone. He recognized a few people. Sarah and her husband were there, and of course, Nadine. He knew she was his grandma, but she hadn't told him to call her that, just like his dad hadn't told him to call him dad.

He wasn't sure what to think about that. It made him feel unsettled, when all he wanted was a place to belong. Was there something he could do that would make them see him as a benefit to their lives? That he wouldn't cause trouble for them?

He thought of his desire to be homeschooled and realized that it wasn't something he should push for. He needed to do what they asked of him. It was the only way to make them not regret that they'd been stuck with him.

Fisting his hands in his sleeves again, Jacob pressed his back against the wall and stared down at the floor. An ache built in his chest, and he wished he was far away from this happy family where he didn't belong. He knew that his mom wasn't coming back, but right then, he would have happily eaten rotisserie chicken at the wobbly table in Lynn's kitchen.

"Hey, man. How's it going?"

A pair of Converse hi-tops came into view, and Jacob blinked rapidly to make sure there were no tears in his eyes before he looked up. A tall guy with dark hair and a smile stood in front of him.

"Hi."

"I'm Rhett," the man said, holding out his hand. "Beau's brother."

Beau... Sarah's husband.

Jacob shook his hand. "I'm Jake."

"Nice to meet you." Rhett moved to stand next to him, leaning back against the wall as he watched people moving around the dining room. "Sarah tells me you like to play video games."

"Yeah. But I can't play any right now."

The guy looked down at him, his brow furrowed. "Why's that? Did Eli ground you or something?"

Jacob hurriedly shook his head. "I haven't done anything wrong."

"Good for you. I used to get in a lot of trouble when I was your age." Rhett grinned as if he was proud of that. "So, if you're not grounded, then why aren't you playing?"

"I used to play with my best friend's stuff. He had an Xbox and a Switch, so he'd let me play on one while he played on the other, but then I moved here."

"So you don't have a console to play on?"

Jacob shook his head. "My uh... Eli... uh... he's let me play some games on his tablet."

Rhett rolled his eyes. "But probably not anything you really want to play, right?"

"It's fine. I probably shouldn't play many video games. I'll be going to school soon, I think."

"What games do you like to play?" Rhett asked.

"Bobby and I usually play Fortnite. We also played Minecraft."

"Ah, yes. I've played both of those."

Jacob relaxed a bit, finding Rhett to be someone who probably wouldn't have any expectations of him. For the next few minutes, they talked about different video games, and for that time, he felt like maybe he belonged.

"Holding up the wall, Rhett?" A man with a broad smile and blonde hair approached them.

"Jake and I are sharing the task."

"Jake, huh?" The man focused on him. "I'm Gavin."

Gavin... Leah's husband.

Jacob held out his hand. "Nice to meet you."

Gavin took his hand in a firm grip. "Nice to meet you, too. How are you liking New Hope?"

"It's nice."

"I can only take it in small doses," Rhett said. "Like a couple of weeks, then I need to head to a big city for a few days."

"You're just a spoiled city boy," Gavin told him with a thump on the arm. "Where did you live before coming here, Jake?"

"Shreveport."

"Louisiana." Gavin nodded as he crossed his arms. "I've been there for a show or two over the years."

"A show?"

"Well, now he's just going to start bragging," Rhett said. "*I'm a famous singer. I'm so talented.* Blah, blah, blah."

Gavin just laughed at the other guy's digs at him. "I only speak the truth."

"Whatever, dude. I still can't figure out why Leah fell for a guy like you."

Jacob listened as the two exchanged good-natured jabs. Neither seemed to take the other too seriously. They were showing a light-hearted side that he hadn't seen yet from his... from Eli. He needed to stop thinking of Eli as his dad until the man showed that he really wanted to be his dad.

There was a bustle of activity around them, and Jacob watched it, spotting the person who was married to Gavin. The unsmiling twin. Only she did smile occasionally. However, her biggest smile was reserved for Gavin when he snagged her as she walked by, drawing her in for a quick kiss before letting her go again.

His mom had had a few boyfriends over the years, but none had treated her very well. The couples he'd seen since coming to New Hope seemed to be good to each other. Though he was glad to see that such a relationship was possible, it also hurt to know that it hadn't happened for his mom. She'd deserved it as much as these people did.

"I think we're ready to eat," Nadine said after getting everyone's attention. "Just look for your name on the table place cards to know where to sit."

Jacob hesitated for a moment before Rhett dropped his arm onto his shoulders. "I know this can be overwhelming. It was the first few times I joined them here."

Thankfully, when he found his name, it was between Eli and Rhett. He took in the platters and bowls of food, sure that it was more than even the group gathered there could eat.

"Once again, I'm so thankful that each of you could join us. We're especially thankful for the youngest among us who are joining us for the first time. Noah and Jacob." She gave Jacob a smile, then turned to the older gentleman sitting beside her. "Greg, would you say thanks for the food, please?"

"I'd be glad to."

As people bowed their heads, Jacob did the same, listening as the older man prayed, giving thanks for the food and the people gathered there.

When the prayer was over, Rhett leaned closer to him and said, "That's my grandfather."

Beau was sitting next to the older man, with Sarah on his other side. Jacob had expected to see just Eli's immediate family and their spouses there. However, it seemed like they opened their home to more than just their own family.

Eli would hold each bowl or platter for Jacob to put some of the contents on his plate before serving himself. Jacob didn't take a lot of food. His mom had always told him to just take a little at first, and once he was finished, then he could take more.

Jacob didn't interact with anyone at the table as he ate. Instead, he just listened to the conversation going on around him. Gavin and Leah talked about the honeymoon trip they'd taken, or rather, Gavin talked about it, with Leah adding very little.

Sarah was definitely more outgoing than Leah, laughing often. In a way, Jacob felt like he was more like Leah, personality-wise. He had never been outgoing, chatting and laughing easily the way some kids did. Those kids were usually the popular ones. Jacob had definitely never been one of those, but Rhett and Gavin probably had been.

It felt weird to be surrounded by so many people, some of whom had known his mom. All of them had been nice to him. But he wasn't sure this was where he belonged.

Anxiety twisted in his stomach, and he was glad that he hadn't taken a lot of food. Right then, he'd be hard pressed to finish even the little he'd taken. He swallowed a couple of times, then lifted a forkful of mashed potatoes to his mouth. Focusing on eating the next few bites, he shut out the conversation flowing around him.

Jacob managed to get most of the food on his plate eaten, but that was going to be all he could do. He didn't bother to take any more food from the dishes on the table, even though others—like Rhett—piled more on their plates.

"Is there something I can pass you?" Eli asked, pulling Jacob's attention from his plate.

"I'm good, thanks." He set his fork down and moved his hands to his lap.

He glanced around the table but didn't catch anyone's eye. Jacob wished he could escape and talk to Bobby. But even that was hard. His friend's life was still pretty much the same. He knew the kids he went to school with. He knew his teachers. His bedroom was still his bedroom, complete with Fortnite posters. And he still had his mom and dad.

While Jacob... all he had was a life of uncertainty, and it was filling him with anxiety. He'd seen his mom riddled with anxiety, and he'd experienced it, mainly at school. But right then, he was coming to understand how crippling it could be.

After losing his mom, he'd clung to the hope that the dad he'd never met would want him. Would offer him a home and the love he'd lost when his mom had died.

He'd been such a fool. *Such* a fool. So far, he felt like even though he had a room in Eli and Anna's home, he didn't have a place in their lives.

"As we do each year, I'd like to give you the opportunity to share what you're thankful for."

Jacob looked at Nadine, her words pulling him from his thoughts. He was supposed to tell them what he was thankful for? Was she kidding?

"No pressure on anyone," Nadine said with a smile. "I know some of you prefer not to share."

Relief filled Jacob, taking his anxiety down a notch, too. Even if he'd felt like he had something to be thankful for, he still wouldn't have felt comfortable talking in front of a group of people who were essentially strangers.

He tried to listen as people around the table talked, sharing what had happened in their lives for which they were thankful. It was surprising that more chose *not* to share than to share. Sarah and Beau shared, as did Leah and Gavin. All of them were thankful for the love they shared with their spouse.

The older man who'd prayed shared first, followed by Nadine did. Rhett didn't say anything, though, nor did the woman who looked like him. He thought her name was Julianna. Most surprising, neither Eli nor Anna spoke up right away.

It wasn't until they didn't jump right in to say what they were thankful for that Jacob realized he'd wanted them to express thanks for *him.*

"I'm grateful that after a difficult pregnancy and long labor, Noah arrived safely and that he's been a healthy baby," Anna said after the others had spoken.

"Yes," Nadine said with a smile. "It's wonderful to have some new faces at the table this year."

Jacob figured that included him, vague as the comment was. Though he might have hoped for more, it was definitely better than nothing. Nadine had already shown him that she was a caring person that day she'd made cookies with him. Even so, he was beginning to feel like there wasn't a place for him in their world.

He wished he could slip out of the lodge and return to the house, even if he had to sit on the porch and wait for them to unlock the door.

Fortunately, Rhett seemed to understand how he felt, and after they'd had dessert, he took Jacob downstairs to the basement, where there was a television. He used his fancy phone to find some movies, scrolling through them until he found one that Jacob hadn't seen, then casting it up onto the large screen.

Jacob breathed a sigh of relief as he settled back on the overstuffed couch. Rhett seemed to understand that Jacob didn't want to talk. He also didn't want to think. He just wanted to escape his life and all its pain for a little while.

CHAPTER TWELVE

Eli finished bringing the last of the Christmas decorations from the storage room. As he set the bin next to the others, he turned to Anna where she sat giving Noah his bottle.

She held up a hand toward him. "Don't even say it. Yes. I want to do this."

"As long as you're sure." He was sort of glad, actually, to see her wanting to do something so... normal. But at the same time, he didn't want her to get overwhelmed, thinking this was something she *had* to do.

"I'm sure. I'll put out some of the decorations today, then we can go get a tree next week and decorate it."

"Sounds like a plan." He was glad that she was interested in doing something she'd always enjoyed prior to Noah's birth. Even the previous Christmas, when she'd been feeling sick most of the time, she'd managed to decorate their house beautifully and had also helped his mom decorate the lodge and cabins.

This would be Noah's first Christmas, and possibly Jacob's first with them also, so it would be nice if it could be as close to normal as possible.

Jacob had helped him carry in the bins, but now he hovered near the hallway leading to the stairs. He'd been withdrawn and quiet since dinner the previous day, and Eli wasn't sure what to do about it. When he'd tried to get him to talk earlier, Jacob had said he was fine. Eli wasn't sure that was the truth, but he could hardly force the boy to talk.

It would be so much easier if he and Anna could come to an agreement on what to do about Jacob. He needed to go to school, but Eli was very hesitant to enroll him without having a definite decision made as to where he would be living. And the uncertainty wasn't good for Jacob, because even though he didn't say anything, he could probably sense that things were up in the air.

This situation wasn't fair to any of them, but that didn't mean that they couldn't work their way through it. Unfortunately, as long as he and Anna couldn't agree on what to do about Jacob, he wasn't sure how to resolve it.

A knock on the door interrupted his thoughts, and Eli frowned. He glanced at Anna, but she just shrugged. No one had said anything about stopping by, but then that had never stopped his family before.

Pulling open the door, he was surprised to see Rhett standing there. "Hey. I didn't know that you even knew where I lived."

"Ha. Very funny," Rhett said with a grin. "I'm actually here to see Jacob. Is he around?"

"Yep. Come on in."

"I hope you don't think I'm overstepping, but I thought maybe I'd have a better idea of what gaming system he could use," he said as he lifted the shopping bag he held.

"You bought Jacob a gaming system?" Eli asked.

"Yeah." Rhett looked wary for a moment. "Was that wrong of me? He said he usually plays video games with his best friend but that he doesn't have a gaming console."

Eli dragged a hand through his hair. "I really didn't think about it, to be honest. I made sure that he could video chat with Bobby, but I didn't consider that they might miss playing games."

"That's because you're old, bro," Rhett said with a grin.

Eli gave an exasperated shake of his head, though he was used to Rhett's personality. The guy flitted in and out of their lives, depending on how fed up he was with small town life. But like a boomerang, the guy always came back again, since Beau had made sure he knew that he always had a home with him and Sarah. Rhett and Sarah actually got along better than Sarah and Julianna, Beau's sister, did.

"Okay. So you brought him an Xbox?"

"Yes, I did," Rhett said. "Along with a couple of... other things."

"Like?"

"A television? Some stuff that works with the Xbox. Maybe a tablet."

Eli frowned. "Does he need all that stuff?"

"I realize you were raised here in the sticks as a teen, but let me assure you that teens of today have all these things. I mean, his buddy apparently has two gaming consoles."

"I'm still not convinced that it's necessary, but I'll let Jacob show you to his room where you can set the stuff up."

"Really?" Rhett grinned. "That's great, dude. I promise, you won't regret it."

"Considering it's an idea you came up with, I almost feel that it's a guarantee that I will." Eli turned to where Jacob stood, cautious hope on his face. "There will be some restrictions on it, though, Jacob. It wouldn't be responsible of me to allow you to just play it all day long."

"I won't," he said. "I promise."

Rhett approached Jacob. "Lead me to your room, young man, and let's get this all set up."

Eli watched the pair head up the stairs, then disappear.

"Are you sure that's a good idea?" Anna asked.

He turned to face Anna. "What do you mean?"

"Giving him internet access in his room."

"I don't know," Eli admitted. "I'll talk to him about it."

"I think this should have been a decision you made, not Rhett."

Eli shrugged. "I had already sort of told him I'd get him a way to keep in contact with his friend. If this stuff helps him deal with his grief, then I'm willing to consider it. At his age, I don't know what else can help him. He's lost everything that's familiar to him, so if playing videos games with his best friend for a little while each day helps him, I'm not sure I have it in me to deny him that."

"I just hope you're not setting him up to expect stuff like this."

"I honestly doubt that will happen. Jacob doesn't strike me as feeling entitled. He hasn't asked for anything since coming here."

Anna nodded, turning her attention to Noah, who had finished his bottle and was squirming to sit up.

Eli waited for her to continue her objections. Instead, she set Noah in his Exersaucer, then moved to look in the bins he'd brought in. "We need to make a decision about things."

She glanced over at him, her face expressionless. "I think you mean *you* need to make a decision."

Did she really feel that he didn't want her input?

He thought about how he really wasn't open to considering any other options for Jacob and realized that perhaps she had a right to feel that way.

"Would this be any different than if we fostered or adopted a child?" he asked. "They wouldn't be related to either of us."

"It's not about him being related to us, and I'm not opposed to either of those things," Anna said as she lifted a smaller box out of one of the bins. "But I would assume that decision to adopt or foster would have been made by the two of us. I don't feel that's the case with this situation."

"You're right," Eli said, dragged his hand down his face. "Of course you are. Decisions like this should be made by both of us."

He waited for her to say something, but she stayed silent as she continued to unpack things from the bin. "Give me some options, Anna. Help me see another solution."

"Answer me this," she said as she looked up to meet his gaze. "If you weren't even in this equation... If they had called Josie instead of you... If you hadn't been listed as his father... What would have happened to him?"

Eli shrugged. "I suppose they would have had to figure it out."

"So why can't that be the way it is now?"

Eli was suddenly weary. How could it be that way now when Jacob thought he was a McNamara, and that Eli was his father? Maybe he should have told the woman who called that there was no way he could be Jacob's father and that they should call Josie instead. But when that thought had crossed his mind during the call, it had left him feeling unsettled.

"Want to give me a hand?" Rhett asked.

He glanced over. "Sure. What do you need?"

"I need some help bringing the television in."

More than happy to escape the heavy atmosphere in the living room, Eli shoved his feet into his shoes and followed Rhett out to the truck he was driving.

"This yours?" he asked as Rhett dropped the tailgate down.

"Yep. You can take the boy out of Texas, but not Texas out of the boy."

"If that's the case, where's your cowboy hat?"

"And mess up this hair? I have to draw the line somewhere."

"Uh..." Eli stared at the box that was lying flat in the bed of the truck. "That's quite a television."

"I know, but I got some great Black Friday sales today. It was just as cheap to get this one as to get a smaller one."

"Yeah, but does Jacob *need* one that big?"

"The bigger, the better."

"Not sure that's true for everything," Eli muttered as he took hold of one side of it.

"Hey, cut me some slack. It's been ages since I've needed to buy some toys. I had a lot of fun buying this stuff."

Eli might have protested the cost, but he knew Rhett could afford it, thanks to his family. He was also pretty sure that Rhett wouldn't ask for the stuff back at some point. For all that Rhett seemed a little juvenile at times, Eli had seen that he was kindhearted and generous.

They carried the television back into the house and up the stairs to the room where Jacob was staying. The teen was sitting on his bed, pulling stuff out of a box.

"This is all so cool," Jacob said, his eyes wide. "Thank you so much, Rhett."

"No problem, buddy. I expect you to get lots of wins."

Jacob grinned. "I'm a pretty good player. My friend Bobby is always the first to be eliminated when we play duos."

"I bet he's missed playing with you, huh?" Rhett asked as he opened the box.

Jacob's smile slipped a bit. "Yeah. He keeps asking when we can play again."

Eli felt a little bad that he hadn't pursued getting him the game console sooner, especially since Jacob had told him they played games together a lot.

Video games hadn't been a huge part of his life, though it wasn't that he'd never played them. However, as a teen, he'd had a lot of other things in his life demanding his attention.

But even as he watched Jacob and Rhett set stuff up, Anna's words rang in his head. Was it right to let Jacob get comfortable here when it might not be where he'd stay?

Maybe the best thing he could do was explain everything to Jacob. The fact that he wasn't his dad. That it was possible that he'd need to go live with Josie or Pete, even though neither of them really had the capability to take him in.

None of that sat well with him, and he didn't know why. From the moment he'd heard about Jacob, he'd felt the need to take care of the boy, and it had nothing to do with his past with Sheila. It might have made more sense if it had.

Everything was just so complicated. Not that he hadn't faced complicated situations before. But in the past few years, especially since Anna's arrival, life had been a bit simpler.

"Well, I'll leave you guys to it," Eli said. "Unless you need my help?"

"I think we're good. Though I'll need your wi-fi password."

"I'll get it for you. I don't know it off the top of my head." Eli went back downstairs and found the notebook where they kept the passwords they needed.

Once he found it, he wrote it on another piece of paper and took it back up to Rhett. He was glad that Jacob had a distraction so that he wasn't around the tension between him and Anna.

"A huge television?" Anna asked when he joined her in the living room again. "It seems very excessive."

"This is Rhett we're talking about. I think all he knows is excessiveness. He probably figures, why buy a small television when he can afford a big one."

"It's ridiculous," Anna said with a shake of her head. "Why didn't you just tell him no?"

"Honestly? I know nothing about current gaming consoles or even televisions. If he can fill that gap for Jacob, then I'm all for it."

"Jacob needs clothes more than he needs video games."

Eli sank down on the couch near Noah's seat. "I'm not so sure about that, actually. Being able to connect with his best friend is probably better for his mental health than new clothes."

"I suppose."

She didn't sound convinced, and Eli couldn't blame her, except he really did think that was true.

When there was another knock on the door, Eli sighed. "When did our home become Grand Central Station?"

"Not sure," Anna said with a glance at the door. "If I had to guess, I'd say Leah and Gavin and maybe Sarah."

Eli got to his feet and went to the door to open it. Sure enough, on the porch stood his two sisters and both their husbands. "C'mon in. Join the party."

"You're having a party?" Sarah asked as she breezed in. "My invite must have gotten lost in the mail. Hey, Anna. Hi, Noah baby. Your favorite aunt is here."

"Yes, she is," Leah said as she knelt beside Noah's Exersaucer.

"Is Rhett here?" Beau asked as he watched his wife vie with Leah for Noah's attention.

"Yep. He showed up with his arms full of everything Jacob needs for gaming."

Beau chuckled. "He did say he was going to do some Black Friday shopping. I just didn't realize what he was shopping for."

"They're upstairs setting it all up."

"I'm gonna go check it out." He pointed at the twins. "Better keep an eye on your baby. One of them might run off with him."

"I'm going with Beau," Gavin said, heading for the stairs. "Be back in a few."

"Are you decorating your tree today?" Sarah asked. "Or maybe not, since you have no tree."

"We're going to get a real one next week, I think."

"Mom said we're decorating tomorrow," Leah said.

Eli sat back down on the couch, watching as Sarah lifted Noah out of his seat. He hoped Anna wouldn't get overwhelmed by having them there. Although they would definitely be a good distraction for her.

"I thought you might have gone Black Friday shopping," Sarah said.

Anna grimaced. "Nope. The only Black Friday shopping I'm going to do is online. I have tons of Christmas gifts left to get."

"Well, you don't have to buy anything for me," Sarah told her. "Just get a picture of Noah with a frame that says *For my favorite auntie.*"

"I guess I could get a couple of those."

"Nope. You only need one," Sarah insisted.

"Well, if I just buy one for Leah, what do I get for you?"

A smile tugged at Eli's lips, and for a moment, he felt lighter, having witnessed Anna's momentary lapse into her old sense of humor. Sadly, he knew it wouldn't last, but he'd take these small moments for the time being and pray that more would come in the future. Next week, she'd be going to her first therapist appointment, and he hoped that she'd get the tools she needed to get back to a place where she was a happier person.

"I love that I'm going to get the best gift ever, and I didn't even have to ask for it," Leah said. "Thanks, Sarah."

"You're both mean," Sarah muttered, then she nuzzled Noah's neck. "But you love me, right, Noah?"

He responded by squealing and bopping Sarah on the face with his hands.

"Now let me hold him for a bit," Leah said. "I've been gone for ages."

Sarah gave Noah another kiss, then handed him over. Now baby-free, she got to her feet and went over to where Anna was setting things out on an end table.

"Can I help?"

Anna glanced over at her. "You can set up the nativity scene if you want."

After giving Sarah a large flat box, Anna pointed her to a shelf in the built-in bookcase that she'd cleared off. Eli pulled up his music app and found a Christmas playlist that Anna had set up the previous year. If they were going to do Christmas stuff, it seemed like they should do it accompanied by some holiday music.

As he watched his sisters with his wife and baby, things seemed almost normal. Almost...

Still, it gave him hope that they'd be able to figure things out and move on to the next chapter of their lives.

CHAPTER THIRTEEN

Anna gripped the steering wheel and stared blankly out the front windshield of her car, drained and exhausted. She hadn't expected the first session would be quite so... intense. When she'd sat down in the comfy chair in the therapist's office, she'd expected the woman to give her a list of things to do, much as the doctor had done.

But there had been more questions. More discussion.

She couldn't ignore the situation anymore, which was a good thing, even though, at the moment, dealing with it left her feeling hollowed out. The therapist hadn't said she should go on medication, but she'd made sure Anna knew it was an option if she felt it necessary.

Right then, Anna wasn't sure what to think about anything. She was beginning to suspect that her depression was complicated by her career. Since meeting Eli and moving to New Hope, she thought she'd come to terms with balancing her desire to appear perfect while also being honest.

For the majority of her career, in her YouTube videos and on her social media, she'd always strived to show a very put-together life. She had a lifestyle and fashion channel, after all. Everything had been done to show the best of her life.

In the time since she and Eli had been married, she'd tried to show a more realistic view of her life. But she couldn't just stop doing the kind of videos that had attracted people to her channel. When she'd gotten a positive pregnancy test, she'd had high expectations for sharing on YouTube about her pregnancy and delivery. All while glowing beautifully.

She'd watched other videos from women whose channels were similar to hers who had had babies, and she'd loved their content. It was what she'd hoped to share with her viewers.

Only it hadn't worked out that way, and each day when she'd woken up still feeling horrible, her mood had dipped more. She felt like she was caught in a vicious cycle. Her depression had robbed her of her ability to function, and her inability to function like she wanted to had pulled her down further into her depression.

Something had to break the cycle, and even though she didn't feel super confident after her first session, maybe the counseling would be the tool she needed.

Now, though, she needed to get home, so that Eli didn't start to worry. Or at least worry more than he already did.

When she got home, Anna discovered that Noah had just gone down for his nap. It was tempting to go lay down herself, but she didn't. Instead, she settled on a stool at the counter in the kitchen.

Jacob was nowhere to be seen, which meant he was most likely up in his room. It was where he spent a good chunk of time. Well beyond the time that Eli had told him he was allowed to be on the Xbox. However, any time she'd walked by his door, it had been open, and he'd been sitting on his bed with a notebook and pencil. Any time Eli asked him to do something, he'd done it without complaint.

But things were still unsettled where he was concerned. It was something else that felt like a vicious cycle. She knew that she should be more open to what Eli wanted for Jacob, but she feared failing one more person in her life. And in her current state of mind, it felt like failure wasn't just a possibility. It was guaranteed.

Eli set a cup of tea on the counter in front of her. "When did you want to go cut down a tree?"

Anna shrugged. "What's the warmest, driest day this week? I don't really want to take Noah out in the cold and wet."

Eli pulled out his phone and tapped the screen. "Looks like that will be tomorrow."

"Then I guess that's when we should go." She lifted the cup and took a sip of the chai tea he'd made for her.

"Are you sure you're up for that?" he asked. "I could just go and buy a tree, so we don't have to hassle the tree farm."

Anna was tempted. It would be a lot easier if she could just stay at the house with Noah and not have to chance that he'd spend the entire trip out to the tree farm screaming his head off. Whether he'd be happy during a car ride these days was anyone's guess.

But if she was going to get her life headed back in the right direction, she needed to do the things that at one time would have brought her joy. And if Noah was unhappy about it, she'd still take pictures and tell him all about it when he was grown up.

She couldn't post those pictures on social media, though, because heaven forbid anyone realize that their Christmas tree outing was anything less than perfect. Part of her knew it would be a step in the right direction to post those pictures, anyway. But that win would only be short term, because she doubted that she'd be able to *leave* them up.

The next afternoon, Anna carried Noah downstairs from his nap. She'd also laid down for a bit, but, unsurprisingly, she hadn't been able to sleep. Once he'd woken from his brief nap, she'd dressed them both in their warmest clothes.

Eli was standing at the window that looked out over the forest that filled the land behind the house. When he didn't turn right away, Anna realized that he must be deep in thought.

"Ready to go?" she asked.

He turned to face her, his expression tense for a moment before he smiled, though it didn't reach his eyes. "Yep. Do you have everything for Noah?"

"And then some," she admitted. "But I don't want to be caught without something we might need."

"I've already put the stroller in," he said as he took Noah from her, then headed to the door.

She followed him, picking up the diaper bag from where she'd left it after she'd finished filling it earlier. He opened the inner door and waited for her to walk out the door before stepping out behind her.

Frowning, she turned to him. "Is Jacob in the car?"

"No." Eli's answer was clipped as he walked past her and down the steps to where the SUV was parked.

"Where is he?"

Eli opened the rear door, then settled Noah in his car seat. "He's with my mom."

"What? Why?"

After shutting the door, Eli turned to face her, an incredulous look on his face. "Why? You really have to ask that?"

Anna felt a bit sick. She hadn't meant... hadn't thought...

"I figured it wouldn't be fair to lead him on, having him go with us when he's not going to be staying. So he's spending some time with my mom. I think they plan to make some Christmas cookies."

There was sadness in his words and on his face. She'd done that. She'd allowed the mess of her emotions to spill over onto a grieving boy. And, of *course*, Eli would take her side. Whether or not he felt it was right, he'd do what he could to accommodate her.

Ever the gentleman, Eli opened her door and waited until she was in her seat before closing it. When he slid behind the wheel, his jaw was clenched, and he didn't look at her.

"We can stop and pick him up," she said softly. "I didn't mean for you to exclude him from this."

"No." Eli started up the engine. "If he's not going to be part of our family, I don't want to offer him a glimpse of what he might have had and then take it all away from him."

"But what about him spending time with your mom? Isn't that doing the same thing?"

Eli shook his head. "Mom would happily spend time with him, even if he had to live somewhere else. I'll contact Josie this week to see if I can meet with her to discuss options for Jacob."

Anna turned to look out the passenger window, blinking back tears that blurred the cabins as Eli drove them out to the main road. It hadn't felt unreasonable to want Jacob to be with his biological family. If he hadn't had any, that might have been different. Or if Eli *had* been his father, she wouldn't have had a reason to feel like this.

And yet, Anna knew that she *still* would have felt like this, even if that were the case. In her current state of mind, she would have resented Eli having had a son with another woman. Her thoughts and emotions felt so irrational and out of her control.

But to some extent, that was a lie. Those emotions might come, but she had a choice about what to do with them. Instead of trusting that God had brought Jacob to them for a reason, all she'd seen was this child barging into their lives when she was already struggling.

Eli had asked her to consider letting Jacob stay with them, but she hadn't, really. All she'd allowed herself to do was to see all the problems with it. How including him would stress their lives even more.

Maybe God had had enough of her insistence on perfection by allowing things into her life that were absolutely beyond her control. And if that was the case, she hadn't learned the lesson He was trying to teach her yet.

She was such a mess, and she knew that the depression she was struggling with had been exacerbated by her issues with unrealistic expectations and the drive to show only perfection to the world.

When Eli pulled into the parking lot of the tree farm, there were hardly any other cars in the lot, which was likely because it was a weekday. Also, people probably weren't out getting their real trees this early in the season.

Anna let out a breath and turned toward Eli, thankful that Noah was quiet. "I'm sorry."

Eli rested his hand on the steering wheel, staring straight ahead for a moment before he glanced over at her. "I know."

"I don't mean to be this way." She hugged herself. "I don't feel like I know who I am anymore. I've... lost myself."

"I can see that, and it hurts to see you struggling. Especially when I know that I've made things worse by agreeing to bring Jacob into our lives." Eli sighed. "I should have realized that we weren't in a good place for that."

"I really just don't think I can be who he needs," Anna said. "I can barely take care of Noah."

"I'm not saying this to force you into anything, but honestly, I'm not sure that Jacob needs anything from you. If Sheila was struggling with mental illness to the extent that suicide became her only choice, I feel like Jacob has probably just been raising himself anyway, especially lately."

And didn't that just make Anna feel worse for her attitude. She needed to think this through. If only she could see where she was going to be in a week or a month. Was she going to get any better?

"I know that you're struggling, but you're not alone. Only you can do the work inside you, in your mind. But with taking care of Noah and everything else, I'm there for you. And so are our family and our friends. You can't do it all yourself, and no one expects you to. Lean on us. Let us play a role in your life."

Tears pricked at her eyes. "I should be able to be a wife, a mother, and a career person without struggling."

"Why?"

"Because everyone else does?"

Eli frowned at her. "Have you *met* everyone else? How do you know that everyone else has done that without struggling?"

"My mom did when she had me."

"She took you to work with her?" Eli asked.

"Well, no. She had a nanny to watch me while she worked." Anna frowned. "But your mom worked, even with twins."

"But she still wasn't alone. She had family who were around her, and from what she's said, she had help from some women at church, who they hired to help with the cleaning and other stuff. She did *not* do it alone. Your mom did *not* do it alone. *You* don't have to do it alone."

Anna sat there for a moment, letting the words sink in. She wanted to grab onto them and hold them close, but there was still a part of her that struggled with the idea of asking people for help.

"Think about it," Eli said. "We'll talk more about how we can help you later. Right now, let's get a Christmas tree."

He opened his door and got out, letting in a rush of cold air. Anna moved more slowly, wishing she felt ready to head into the season that was usually her favorite time of the year. Maybe getting a tree up and decorated would help.

By the time she joined him, Eli had the stroller out of the back and was putting Noah into it. She tucked the diaper bag into the basket underneath the seat, then Eli pushed it toward the entrance of the farm.

The stroller had big wheels, so it handled the rutty paths at the farm with no problem. In the past, she would have been determined to get the best tree on the farm, even if it took hours to find.

This time, however, she wasn't looking for that perfect tree. She just wanted a tree that would look okay in the spot in the living room where they would put it. Eli, however, vetoed a couple of the trees that she'd been prepared to settle for.

In the end, after they'd wandered around for about half an hour, they found a tree that was pretty, even if it wasn't completely symmetrical. Eli took Noah out of the stroller and stood with him in front of the tree for a picture—at his insistence. Then he asked the guy who came to cut the tree to take a picture of the three of them in front of it.

Noah looked cute in his beanie, thick jacket, and little runners. He smiled readily enough for the pictures, although he wasn't happy to be put back in the stroller.

"Are you up for dinner at Mom's?" Eli asked as they drove back toward the lodge.

Her first response was to say *no*, but Anna knew that she needed to at least try to interact with people. Used to be that she'd loved to go to dinner at the lodge with the family and whatever guests might be around. But lately... being around people who knew her so well was hard. She couldn't keep hiding away, however, hoping she'd be able to get her life together first.

"Okay. I guess we should take the tree home first, though."

"Yeah. We'll set it up and then head over."

"We don't have to bring anything?"

"Nope. Mom said just to come if we felt up to it."

It was tempting to take the out that Nadine had offered, but she couldn't. These were the little steps she had to take. Everyone who would be there loved her and supported her, so it was a safe place for her to be.

At the house, she had to put a fussing Noah into his Exersaucer so she could help Eli get the tree into the house and set up in its spot in the living room. Once that was done, they headed down to the lodge.

A spicy, tomatoey aroma greeted them, which meant they were probably having lasagna. Her stomach rumbled in appreciation, and she was glad she'd agreed to come, even if it was just for the food.

The lodge felt like home almost as much as their house did. She'd spent a wonderful time there when she first came to New Hope, and it had been where she'd fallen in love with Eli. It was where a new chapter of her life had begun. She needed to accept that this was yet another new chapter in her life, and that it didn't need to be a perfect chapter.

She just had to accept that God would write it in a way to bring glory to Himself, instead of how she'd been trying to live things. Or *not* live, which was more accurate to how things had been lately.

One step at a time.

She might not be able to see very far down the road, but she realized that she didn't need to. She just needed to put one foot in front of the other, trusting that God could see what was still to come, even though she couldn't.

CHAPTER FOURTEEN

"You've done a wonderful job, Jacob."

Jacob looked up at the older woman as they stood side by side at the counter with two pans of cooked lasagna in front of them. "I hope it tastes okay."

She put her arm around his shoulders and squeezed, the light scent of her perfume briefly replacing the aroma of the lasagna. "It's going to taste just fine."

He didn't know why Eli had dropped him off at the lodge, and he hadn't been sure what to expect when he'd walked in. For a moment, he'd felt lost and like even though he'd tried his best not to be a burden, he'd become too much for Eli and Anna, and they'd needed time away from him.

"I bet it's going to taste better than anything Sarah has made," Leah said as she smiled at him. For some reason, Leah's smile warmed him. She might not smile much, but she'd smiled at *him*.

When Sarah came to stand next to Leah, Jacob expected her to protest her sister's words. Instead, she said, "Oh, that's probably true. I'm a terrible cook."

"Do you like to cook, Jacob?"

He shrugged. "I've only made stuff like mac and cheese and ramen. I can also make tuna sandwiches. But nothing like this."

"Well, you have an excellent teacher in Mom. She taught me everything I know," Leah said. "She tried to teach Sarah too, but she just burns everything."

"I have so many other things I'd rather be doing. I get distracted."

This was his first time—aside from the cookies—to make something that was actually supposed to taste good. He had really enjoyed it, and he hoped he could cook again soon.

"I want you to think of what else you might like to cook, and next time we'll make that."

Next time. Never had those words carried so much weight. He wanted to cling to them, but he let them go. There was a big chance it would never happen again, but it was still a nice thought.

"And you made a cake too?" Sarah asked.

"Yeah. A chocolate one."

"I can't wait to taste it because I love chocolate."

"I hope it's okay."

"It will be," Nadine said. "You put all the right ingredients in, so I'm sure it will be fine."

A few minutes later, Jacob had just finished putting glasses on the table like Nadine had asked when he heard the front door open. He paused, looking over at the doorway that opened into the foyer.

When he saw it was Beau and Gavin, he turned his attention back to the table. There were places set for Eli and Anna, but he'd heard Nadine tell Sarah and Leah that she wasn't sure they'd be there.

He'd enjoyed the afternoon he'd spent with Nadine, but he still didn't think he fit there. Or maybe it was that he wasn't sure there was a place for him there. But until they told him to go somewhere else, he'd try his best to live in the moment... for however long it lasted.

Once the glasses were all in place, he drifted back to the kitchen, hovering in the background as he waited for someone to tell him what to do next. He watched as the guys hugged their wives and gave them kisses. Everyone had a place. They each belonged there.

Crossing his arms over his chest, Jacob went to the window that looked out over the trees. He liked the trees. He liked being surrounded by them instead of rundown apartment blocks. He wished he could go for a walk by himself, because maybe out in the forest, he'd finally feel like he belonged.

"How's it going, buddy?"

Jacob turned to see Gavin beside him. "It's fine."

"I hear you helped make supper."

"Lasagna, yeah. It might not taste good."

"Hey now," Gavin said, placing a hand on his shoulder. "Don't sell your abilities short, and even if it isn't great, it will still be better than if Sarah had made it."

Jacob gave a huff of laughter. "Yeah, so I heard."

"Regardless, I'm sure it will be just fine. Nadine is a great cook, and she wouldn't have taught you wrong." Gavin grinned. "The big question is, did you enjoy cooking?"

"I did. It was fun."

"Maybe you'll be a chef someday."

Jacob seriously doubted that. The only future he saw in cooking was flipping burgers at a fast-food joint. He wouldn't be able to afford college, let alone chef-school or whatever it was called. All he wanted was to be able to cook food for himself that tasted good.

"What would you like to be when you grow up?" Gavin asked.

Jacob grimaced at the question. How did he explain that he had never been sure he'd have much of a future? He'd always figured that his main job would be taking care of his mom. He'd assumed he'd get a job that would provide enough money to pay the bills and buy food, but he hadn't thought about having a career of any sort.

Even though his mom was gone, he still hadn't thought about a career. How could he look to the distant future when he couldn't even see the immediate future?

"I don't know," he said. "Haven't figured that out yet."

"You still got some time," Gavin told him.

"When did you know you wanted to be a singer?"

Gavin laughed. "I didn't have a choice. I was probably two or three when my dad put a microphone in my hand for the first time, and I sang *Jesus Loves Me* in front of a crowded church."

"Why were you singing so young?"

"My family had a singing group, but I left it a few years back to start my own group."

"That's cool."

"It has its moments," Gavin said. "But at the end of the day, I wouldn't want to be doing anything else. Good or bad, it's what I love to do."

Jacob figured it was good to have a career that made a person feel that way. He had no idea what that might be for him. Part of him was too scared to even think about it because who knew where he'd be when he was Gavin's age?

"Hey! There's my favorite little nephew," Sarah exclaimed.

Jacob's heart clenched, knowing the words weren't directed at him, and for a moment, he wanted to cry. But he didn't. He didn't turn around or acknowledge that he'd even heard the words.

"Do you travel a lot?" he asked, trying to keep his voice steady. "Like go on tours?"

"We go on tours, but we try not to be away from home for too long. Leah's place is here, helping her mom run the lodge, so I don't like to be gone from her too long."

"She doesn't go with you?"

"Sometimes she does, but usually only to the locations that are close by."

Jacob took a breath, tightening his arms around himself as Nadine called for them to all sit down at the table. Gavin looped an arm over his shoulders and walked beside him into the dining room. Rather than let him try to figure out where to sit, the man guided him to a seat, then grabbed the one next to him.

Eli and Anna sat across the table from him, with Noah between them. It was a family unit that he was coming to realize he had no part of, even if Eli was his dad.

"This is great, buddy," Gavin said, nudging Jacob with his elbow. "Why aren't you eating it?"

"Not hungry," he mumbled as he glanced at the man.

He saw concern in Gavin's gaze, so he looked away. With a sigh, he picked up his fork and took a bite. Gavin might have said it tasted good, but to Jacob, it was tasteless. Still, he kept eating, determined not to draw attention to himself.

Maybe it was time for him to make some decisions for himself. He didn't care about all the stuff that was in the room he used at Eli's house. He'd rather live without it than be in a place where he wasn't wanted. Though he honestly wasn't sure there was a place anywhere that he *was* wanted.

Once the meal was over, he quietly helped clear the table. When Noah started to fuss, he accepted a hug from Nadine and a squeeze around his shoulders from Gavin, then left with Eli and Anna. Noah didn't stop crying during the brief trip home.

As they walked into the house, Jacob noticed the undecorated Christmas tree in the corner of the room and realized where they'd been. Feeling like his body was just one big ball of pain, he said goodnight, then headed straight up to his room.

He didn't bother to turn on a light, just closed the door, then went into the small, attached bathroom. Pressing his back against the door, he slid down to sit on the tile floor. He pulled his legs up and wrapped his arms around them.

His grief and pain poured out of him in sobs that he couldn't control. He missed his mom so much. Why did she have to leave him? Why couldn't she have fought harder for him? Why couldn't she have seen how hard it would be for him to be left behind? It had been the two of them for so long, and it could have been the two of them forever. If only she'd wanted to stay with him.

When the tears finally eased, Jacob slowly got to his feet and brushed his teeth, then changed into his pajamas. Wearily, he climbed into bed, wishing he didn't feel so tired. So worn out. So alone.

As he lay there in the darkness, his heart aching with grief, he tried to focus on the happy times he'd had with his mom. They'd definitely had some, even if they'd been few and far between. He let the memories fill his thoughts and follow him into sleep, hoping he'd have happy dreams instead of sad ones.

~*~

Eli leaned against the doorframe of Noah's door, his usual spot to wait and make sure that the baby was actually asleep. When they'd gotten home, he'd sent Anna off to take a bath and go to bed. He'd focused on getting Noah ready for bed, giving him a bath and then his bottle.

It had taken longer than he'd hoped, but finally, Noah was out. Now Eli wanted to spend a few minutes talking with Jacob before it was time for him to go to sleep. He hadn't talked to him at the lodge, so he wanted to make some time before the day was over for them to have a chat.

He walked down the short hall to Jacob's room. Usually, Jacob's door was left open a crack, but right then it was closed. Eli knocked lightly on the door, then waited a moment before opening it.

Expecting to find the light on, Eli paused when he realized the only illumination in the room came from the nightlight he'd given Jacob when he'd first arrived. He pushed the door open a bit more, then approached the bed, where he could see a lump under the covers.

As he stared down at the sleeping boy, Eli felt more strongly than ever that Jacob's place was with them, but the situation seemed impossible. He had no idea how to make it happen.

Anna may have realized that her attitude wasn't great when it came to Jacob, but her admitting that hadn't changed anything. She still didn't feel capable of having someone else in their lives.

Jacob hadn't been a difficult addition to their lives. In fact, he was fairly easy-going. But that didn't mean he wasn't dealing with a mess of things inside, but rather that he was just choosing not to show it. He was pretty sure that Jacob needed to see a professional to help him with his grief, but Eli wasn't sure where to turn for that help.

It occurred to him then that perhaps he could approach Ryker Bennet, who was a pediatrician by training, to see if he was practicing. If he was, maybe he could give Jacob a physical check-up and also recommend a child psychologist for him to see.

Eli gently rested his hand on Jacob's head. *Dear Heavenly Father, please bless Jacob and assure him of Your love for him. Help me know how best to help him and walk beside him through his grief. If it's Your will for him to be with our family, please make it clear to me and to Anna. If it's not, give me clear guidance on where he should go and prepare each of us for that. In Jesus' name, amen.*

As he left the room, he pulled the door almost closed, then headed downstairs. Since it wasn't super late, he decided to give Michael Reed a call.

"Hey, Eli," Michael said when he answered. "How's it going?"

"It's been better," Eli admitted as he pulled a mug from the metal mug tree. He began to make himself a cup of coffee, even though he probably shouldn't be having one this late in the day. However, he needed to do a little work, so if the coffee kept him awake, all the better.

"Lani mentioned that Leah shared a bit about what's been going on."

"We've been struggling a bit," Eli admitted, then shared everything that had happened with Sheila, Jacob, and Anna. He knew Michael would keep what he told him to himself.

Once his coffee was made, he carried the mug and the baby monitor into his workshop. He closed the door, then put Michael on speakerphone and set the phone on the workbench.

"I sure understand how Anna might be struggling," Michael said. "I constantly felt like I was failing Vivi, especially when I had to turn over so much of her care to Lani when I broke my leg. But then I realized that accepting help was the best thing for her. It also made me a better dad, which directly benefitted her."

"I just hate seeing Anna struggle, and then having the situation with Jacob dropped into our laps hasn't helped."

"What are you going to do?" Michael asked.

Eli sighed, his shoulders slumping as he stared down at the piece of wood he was supposed to be working on. "I have no idea. I feel strongly that Jacob should stay with us. That he's meant to be part of our family. Unfortunately, Anna doesn't have that same feeling, and all she sees is how she's already failing at being a wife to me and a mother to Noah, and she doesn't want to let someone else down."

"I wish I had some advice for you, but clearly it's not something I've ever dealt with."

"I just feel so torn. I can't meet the needs of one without sacrificing the needs of the other."

"And Anna won't consider keeping Jacob at all?"

"That's the thing. I think if I put my foot down and said that he was staying, she wouldn't object, but it would damage our relationship. I need her support in this."

"I will certainly be praying for you both as you deal with this."

"I appreciate it," Eli said. "I also wanted to ask you about Ryker. Is he practicing?"

"Yep. Did you want him to see Jacob?"

"I think it would be a good idea to have him checked out. I doubt Sheila took him for regular physicals. Plus, I would like Ryker's recommendation for a therapist for Jacob to help him deal with his grief and everything else going on."

"I'm sure Ryker would be more than happy to help you." Michael gave him Ryker's personal and work contact information. "Or if he can't, I'm sure he'd recommend someone who could."

"Thanks. I appreciate the info."

Michael offered to pray for him, so they spent a couple of minutes in prayer before Eli ended the call. He felt more at peace as he hung up the phone, thankful that he could rely on his friends for support.

In recent months, he and Anna's attendance at the Bible study had been sporadic at best. He missed having it at their place, but it had gotten to be too much for Anna when she was struggling with her pregnancy.

Their life had changed in so many ways since Anna had gotten pregnant. Though he understood that change was inevitable when adding to their family, there were times he missed the ease and predictability of their life prior to Noah's birth. He certainly didn't wish Noah away at all, but he just needed their new phase of life to fall into place a bit better. They were definitely struggling to find their footing as parents and as a family.

He loved Anna, regardless, which was why it was impossible for him to just tell her that Jacob was staying. Their relationship was too important to him to do that. He just prayed that she'd come around and see for herself that Jacob's place was with them.

But if that didn't happen soon, he'd need to figure out another option, even if doing that would inflict further pain on Jacob when he was already hurting with grief. The very thought made Eli's heart ache.

Please, God, help me find the answer to this dilemma that doesn't lead to more hurt for Jacob or Anna.

CHAPTER FIFTEEN

Anna poured some pancake batter onto the griddle. She'd had a decent night, but it had come at the cost of Eli's sleep. He'd kept Noah's monitor with him while he'd worked late into the night in his workshop. She knew that he'd fallen behind in his work while dealing with her and the situation with Jacob.

When Noah had woken earlier, she'd had no trouble getting up with him. She'd felt relaxed after her bath the previous night, and she'd had the best sleep she'd had in ages. It was kind of surprising, considering the day hadn't exactly been easy.

"Can I help you with anything?" Jacob's question drew her attention from the pancakes to where he hovered at the end of the counter. His hair was brushed, and he wore a long sleeve T-shirt that, once again, swam on his thin frame.

Noah squealed and bounced in his Exersaucer where she'd put him after giving him his bottle. Jacob turned toward him with a smile and lowered himself down to Noah's level.

"Good morning, Noah." Jacob reached out and poked at one of the toys on the plastic ring, setting it dancing and making Noah squeal and wave his hands with a grin on his chubby face.

Jacob played with him for a couple of minutes, then got back up and turned to her. "Is there something I can help with?"

"Have you made pancakes before?"

"Just once," he said, then frowned. "But I burned a couple of them."

"I seem to burn at least a couple whenever I make them." She held the spatula out to him. "Do you want to flip these?"

After a moment's hesitation, he took the spatula from her and moved toward the griddle. "Are these ready to flip?"

"Once bubbles start to form on the top, you can use the spatula to lift the edge and see what it looks like on the bottom."

Jacob glanced at her, his brow furrowed before he tentatively slipped the edge of the spatula under the pancake. He tilted his head as he peered at the bottom of the pancake.

"I think it's ready," he said.

"Okay. Now slide the spatula underneath it."

He bit his lip as he carefully pushed the spatula underneath the pancake. Once he had it in place, he looked at her.

"Now flip it."

He hesitated, but then he lifted the pancake and tried to flip it over. It landed partially on the edge of the pancake beside it, and he froze, staring down at the pan.

"That happens to me too," she said. "Let me show you how to fix it."

He handed the spatula back to her and stepped to the side. Anna quickly showed him how to get the pancake moved, then handed the spatula back to him.

"You want me to keep doing it?" he asked. "I kinda messed up."

"It was nothing that couldn't be fixed, and you'll never learn if you don't keep trying."

While he focused on the pancakes, she mashed up a banana for Noah's breakfast, then got out the syrup.

Normally, she found it a bit frustrating to have someone in the kitchen with her, but Jacob was small enough that she could move around without constantly bumping into him. She wondered if Noah would like to help in the kitchen as he got older. When she'd been Jacob's age, she hadn't spent much time in the kitchen, but that was mainly because neither of her parents had been into cooking.

Keeping an eye on Jacob, Anna continued to get breakfast ready. Given that he'd had such a late night, she didn't expect that Eli would be down soon, though it was possible he'd set an alarm. She hoped he hadn't because he needed the sleep as much as she did these days.

When it was time to pour more batter on the griddle, she had Jacob do it, just offering him a little bit of guidance. He seemed to be a quick learner, which made her wonder how he did in school.

"Do you like school?" she asked, letting her curiosity get the better of her.

He stood with his head bent for a moment, then glanced at her. "I don't mind the schoolwork much. But the kids can sometimes be... mean."

"Were you bullied at your old school?" The very idea of it made Anna feel a little sick. She knew that if anyone bullied Noah, she'd become a mama bear.

Jacob looked back down at the pancakes and nudged one of them with the spatula. He gave a shrug but didn't look at her. "They liked to tease me because I'm smaller and because my clothes didn't fit really well."

"If that happens again at your next school, you need to tell someone."

"No one listens," he murmured.

Anna stared at the boy, feeling a wave of sympathy for him. She'd always had a very safe home life. No matter what else was going on in her world, she knew that when she walked through the door of her home, she was safe. Her parents loved her, and though they weren't the most hands-on parents, they had always made sure that she knew they were there for her.

Given that Sheila had committed suicide, Anna could only assume that the home life that Jacob had experienced hadn't been a safe or secure one. She felt for the boy, and suddenly realized how important it was for him to have a safe, stable home. Could they give that to him?

She wanted to say yes, but she just wasn't sure that she was in a good enough place to be a mother to a grieving teenage boy.

"Do you want to put some chocolate chips into the last of the batter?" Anna asked.

"I like them with chocolate chips," Jacob replied as he carefully flipped the pancakes on the griddle.

Anna got the bag from the cupboard and dumped some into the remaining batter. "That should be enough."

Jacob continued to focus on the pancakes, while Anna poured herself a cup of coffee now that it was ready. After doctoring it to her taste, she took a sip, sighing in appreciation.

Noah fussed in his seat, so she set her coffee down and picked him up. Taking him close to where Jacob stood at the griddle seemed to make him happy.

"Are you going to make pancakes someday, Noah?" Jacob asked as he glanced at the baby with a smile, then he looked up at her. "Does he get to eat pancakes?"

"Not yet," Anna told him. "He's just starting to eat solid foods, which means he's eating pureed or mashed stuff. Most of the time, he eats rice cereal and mashed bananas."

"Sorry you don't get to eat these pancakes," Jacob said as he leaned close to Noah for a moment. "But I'm sure you'll love them when you're finally able to have them."

Noah gave a squeal in response, and Anna found herself smiling and enjoying the moment in a way she hadn't enjoyed many lately.

"Something smells good." Eli's rumbling voice had them all turning.

Noah shrieked and held out his arms. With a smile, Eli took Noah from Anna. He bent to give her a kiss. "Sleep well?"

"I did. You should still be sleeping."

"I'm fine." Though he didn't look as exhausted as she'd seen him at times lately, he still looked like he could use another hour or two of sleep.

He moved over to where Jacob stood, his head bent as he stared at the pancakes. Eli rested a hand on his shoulder. "Good morning, Jacob. Are you fixing breakfast for us this morning?"

"I didn't make the batter. I'm just cooking them."

"Well, flipping them is a pretty important part of the process," Eli said. "I'm not sure about you, but I think drinking my pancakes would be pretty gross."

Jacob gave a quiet huff of laughter. "Yeah. It would be."

"We'll be ready to eat in a couple of minutes," Anna said. "Do you want to feed Noah his bananas and cereal?"

"Oh, fun," Eli said. "Ready to give yourself a facial, Noah?"

While he fastened Noah into his highchair, Anna carried over the bowl she'd prepared for him. After handing it to Eli, she returned to the kitchen to get the fruit she'd cut up. She also grabbed the coffee carafe, sure that Eli was going to need the caffeine hit.

"They're all done," Jacob said as he set the spatula down on the counter beside the griddle.

"Nice. Thank you."

"Should I bring them?"

Anna nodded, then went back to the table where she poured Eli his coffee. He lifted it right away and took a sip.

"Amazing. Thanks, sweetheart."

Once they were seated at the table, Eli said a quick prayer, then they began to eat. Jacob took just one pancake and a couple of strawberries. He poured a small amount of syrup on the pancake, then took a bite. As they ate, Noah was the most vocally interactive... with them *and* with his food.

In the past, Anna would have spent her breakfast planning out her day, making a list of everything she hoped to accomplish. Now, she was afraid to make a list because it would consist mainly of *feed*

Noah and *change Noah's diaper*, interspersed with *do the laundry* and *wash the dishes*.

At least she wouldn't have to make a new list each morning, since every day was pretty much the same now. When she'd mentioned that to her therapist, her suggestion had been to make that list, but then add one item that related to just her. It could be something like *take a bubble bath* or *read a chapter in a book*.

She hadn't done that yet, but maybe it was time to give it a try. Her biggest fear was that she'd make her list and then fail to get anything on it done beyond what related to Noah. It used to be that she took pride in being able to cross all the items of her daily to-do list.

Once breakfast was finished, Jacob helped to clear the table. Eli took Noah upstairs to get him cleaned up and dressed for the day.

When Eli came back downstairs, he put Noah in his seat in the living room, then asked Jacob to stay with him.

"Will you be okay on your own for a bit today?" he asked when he joined Anna in the kitchen.

"Uh... sure? What's going on?"

"I called Ryker earlier to make an appointment for Jacob to see him."

Anna glanced over to where Jacob knelt in front of Noah. "Is something wrong?"

"I don't think so, but I think it wouldn't hurt to have him checked over. The main reason I'm taking him, though, is to see if Ryker can suggest a therapist for him."

She hadn't really considered that Jacob might need someone to talk to, but now that Eli mentioned it, it made sense. "Okay. I'll be fine."

"I could drop you at the lodge if you wanted to hang out with Mom and Leah."

Anna's first instinct was to say *no*, but maybe she should spend some time outside of the house. "Sure."

Eli's brows lifted. "Really?"

"I know you thought I'd say no, but I'm trying to do better. I think it will be a good thing."

"Definitely a good thing," Eli said. "I know Mom would love to spend time with you and Noah."

"And it would give Leah a boost as favorite aunt."

Eli chuckled. "So you're Team Leah?"

Anna shrugged. "Just giving her opportunities to catch up since she's been away."

"While you're there, maybe you should escape to one of the rooms and spend some time doing something for yourself, since Mom and Leah would happily take care of Noah."

Anna wasn't sure if she'd take Eli's suggestion, but she put her planner and tablet in the diaper bag. Just in case.

"Jacob," Eli said as he walked toward the boys. "We're going to go see a doctor friend of mine."

Jacob got to his feet, a frown on his face. "A doctor? Why?"

"Did your mom ever take you to a doctor in Shreveport?"

The teen shook his head. "If we needed something, there was a clinic we went to."

"I think it would be a good idea for you to have a check-up. Just to make sure that everything is okay."

Jacob didn't look convinced, but he nodded. Anna got the diaper bag ready to go with bottles and formula, then went to find her planner and tablet. When she came back down, Jacob had his hoodie on, and stood near the door with his hands in his pockets and his head bent.

She and Eli needed to have a serious conversation about Jacob. One that ended in a decision. Not just leaving it hanging like they had every other time.

When Eli pulled to a stop in front of the lodge, Anna opened her door and got out.

"I'll be back out in a couple of minutes, Jacob," Eli said. "You can move to the front seat."

Eli got Noah out, then the two of them walked up the steps and went into the lodge.

Nadine greeted them enthusiastically. "I'm so glad you've come to spend some time with me. It's so quiet around here these days."

Eli handed Noah to his mom as Anna set the diaper bag on the counter. "Leah not here yet?"

"She and Gavin will be here in a few minutes."

"I don't imagine Jacob and I will be gone more than a couple of hours."

"I'll have some lunch ready for you when you get back," Nadine said.

"Thanks, Mom." Eli bent to give Anna a kiss. "Enjoy your time."

"I'll try."

After he left, Anna settled on a stool at the counter, watching as Nadine danced around the kitchen with Noah. The movement made him giggle and squeal, and for a moment, Anna felt like a failure once again because that wasn't something she did with him.

In spite of what she'd gone through in her own life, Nadine's joy always seemed to be near the surface, bursting forth at a moment's notice. Anna felt like hers was buried so deep as to be nearly unreachable. They were all blessed to have Nadine in their lives, since she was more than happy to share her joy with them.

"How are you feeling?" Nadine asked as she came and laid an arm across Anna's shoulders and gave her a squeeze.

"Not too bad. Eli was a sweetheart and took the night shift with Noah, which meant that I got some decent sleep."

"That's wonderful." Nadine walked around the counter and turned on the kettle. "Would you like a cup of coffee or some tea?"

"Some tea would be nice."

Nadine confidently balanced Noah on her hip as she pulled down cups and her stash of assorted teas. She set the decorated box in front of Anna. "Pick a flavor."

Anna wasn't a real tea connoisseur, but she did have certain flavors she liked. That day, she chose a chai tea. To her, it perfectly complemented that time of year, with autumn easing into Christmas. The dreary day also seemed to demand the spicier flavors.

When Nadine set the hot tea in front of her, Anna picked the cup up and inhaled the aroma, sighing in appreciation. "Thank you."

"You're very welcome, darling."

Leah arrived a couple of minutes later, bringing with her a bakery box from her aunt's restaurant in New Hope. "I come bearing muffins!"

"Where's Gavin?" Nadine asked as she gave Leah a one-armed hug.

"He's still in the car on a call with the guys. It's his first since we got back." Leah took Noah from her mom and gave him a kiss on the cheek. "I think they're discussing some upcoming concerts."

Leah came over and sat down next to Anna, leaning against her arm for a moment. "How's it going?"

"It's going okay. How about with you?"

Leah smiled. "It's going really well."

Anna was glad to hear that, especially considering she and Gavin were newly married. She remembered how wonderful those early months were. Not that she was unhappy with her marriage to Eli, but the responsibilities in their lives currently meant they couldn't just focus on each other the way they had in the months following their wedding.

"Do you mind watching Noah for a bit?" Anna asked. "I'd like to use one of the rooms to do some work."

"I don't mind at all," Nadine said. "I think that's an excellent idea."

"Thank you." Anna felt a small surge of excitement as she pulled her planner and tablet from the diaper bag. "His bottles and formula are in the diaper bag. The formula is pre-measured for the amount of water in the bottles. He should be okay for a bit, though."

Leaving Noah to go to a different part of the lodge didn't feel as wrong as when she left the house completely. Being close by in case he needed her was important.

She chose the room she'd stayed in when she'd just been getting to know Eli and his family. Wandering around the room, she let her fingertips trail over the furniture before coming to a stop in front of the window. She'd done videos in front of that window, taking advantage of the natural light.

There would be no videos that day. But maybe what she did in the room that morning would help her get back on track. Her family needed that from her, and she needed that for herself.

CHAPTER SIXTEEN

Jacob stared at the man sitting on a rolling stool in front of him and Eli. He had a friendly smile and chatted easily with Eli. Clearly, they knew each other.

"How are you finding being back?" Eli asked with a gesture at the room.

The man's smile grew. "It's been great. Of course, I'm taking it slow. I'm still working with Michael for the time being, splitting my time between him and the clinic."

"Busy man."

"Yep. Quite the juggling act, since I need to make sure that I still have time for Sophia and Bryson, too."

"Well, I'm glad we were able to catch you here today."

"I'm glad too." The man turned to Jacob and held out his hand. "Hi. My name is Ryker Bennet."

"I'm Jacob."

"It's nice to meet you, Jacob. So, what brings you by today?"

Jacob looked at Eli, then shrugged. "I'm not sure."

Ryker turned his attention back to Eli and lifted a brow. "What's up?"

"Jacob's mom recently passed away, and he's come to stay with me. I just wanted him to have a check-up to make sure that he's doing okay."

Jacob wondered if Eli would send him away if they found something wrong with him. Maybe he was just making sure he was getting a healthy kid. Jacob didn't think there was anything wrong with him, except maybe there was a reason he was shorter and skinnier than most the boys his age.

Over the next few minutes, the doctor asked him a bunch of questions, and Jacob did his best to answer them. After he weighed and measured him, he had Jacob sit on the raised bed. He checked his ears, then listened to his heart and lungs.

When the doctor sat back down on his rolling stool, he smiled at Jacob. "Everything looks great. I would suggest that you try to eat a bit more. I'm not talking junk food, but good, healthy food. You're probably going to hit a growth spurt in the next year or two, so it would be good to have decent eating habits in place."

Jacob had no idea if he'd be able to eat better because who knew where he was going to end up. Still, he nodded as he tugged his shirt down. "I'll try."

"Excellent." Ryker glanced at Eli. "Did you have any specific concerns?"

"Not health-wise, no," Eli said. "But I wonder if you might have a recommendation for a therapist."

Ryker's brows lifted slightly, then he turned to Jacob. "Would you like to have someone to talk to?"

"To talk to?" Jacob asked, uncertain what that meant exactly.

Eli got up and laid a hand on his shoulder. "You've been through a lot lately, especially with how your mom died. I thought you might like to have someone who isn't close to the situation to talk to about all of it."

Jacob wasn't sure he'd feel comfortable doing that, but he should probably agree, just to be safe. Especially since it seemed like it was something that Eli wanted him to do. "I guess that might be okay."

"My fiancée's son has been going to someone who has been a big help to him. I think she'd be good for you too, Jacob. She works specifically with kids."

Jacob nodded, because he wasn't sure what else to say.

Ryker turned his attention to Eli. "I'll send you her information, and you and Jacob can talk about what you want to do."

"Thanks, Ryker. I really appreciate this."

When both men got to their feet, Jacob slid off the table and shoved his hands into the pockets of his jeans, hitching them up.

"It was nice to meet you, Jacob," Ryker said. "If anything comes up with your health, just let Eli know, and he'll bring you in to see me."

"Okay."

Eli rested his hand against Jacob's back and guided him out of the small room. "Talk to you later, Ryker."

"You bet, and I'll text you the information for the therapist."

It was raining and chilly as they left the building, so Jacob jogged alongside Eli to get to the SUV. Once they were inside, Eli turned it on and cranked up the heat.

"Did you think there was something wrong with me?" Jacob asked.

Eli glanced at him with a frown. "Not at all. Most kids have a yearly check-up, and since you hadn't, I thought it would be a good idea to get that for you. Noah also gets regular check-ups. It's a way to make sure that any issues that might come up are dealt with right away. Thankfully, it looks like you're doing fine."

His health hadn't been something he'd thought much about. The sickest he could ever remember being was with the flu a couple of years earlier. Otherwise, he caught a cold every once in a while, but nothing more serious.

As Eli drove the SUV from the parking lot, Jacob stared out the window, his thoughts a jumbled mess about everything that had taken place in the past hour. He really wanted to believe that Eli had taken him to the doctor because he cared. But a larger part was positive it had been because he wanted to know what he was getting into with Jacob.

"Do you think I should talk to someone?" Jacob asked. "Do you think I'm crazy? Like my mom?"

"Your mom wasn't crazy, Jacob," Eli said without hesitation. "She likely had a mental illness, much like her mom has. People with mental illnesses aren't crazy, and they can function just fine if they get the help they need."

"Do I have a mental illness?"

"I don't know, but that's not why I want you to see a therapist." Eli fell quiet for a moment as he drove through the traffic. "You've been through a lot, Jacob. More than most kids your age. I know you're grieving for your mom, and I think a therapist could help you work through all that."

Jacob wondered if the therapist could help heal the constant throbbing ache in his heart. He'd assumed that it would always be there, but maybe there was someone who could help him make it hurt a little less.

"If you really don't want to talk to a therapist, I'm not going to force you," Eli told him. "You think about it and let me know."

And if it took him a few weeks to think about it, would he still be with Eli and Anna? Or would they have passed him on to someone else by then?

"Okay." What else could he say?

There was *so* much that he wanted to say, but he kept it inside because he doubted anyone wanted to hear it. But if someone was being paid to listen to him, then maybe he'd be able to let it all out. Perhaps Eli understood that, which was why he was suggesting the therapist.

When they got back to the lodge, lunch was waiting for them. Mindful of what the doctor had said about eating better, Jacob tried to eat a whole bowl of the soup Nadine had made for them. It was rich and tasty, and he even ate a piece of thick bread.

No one asked about the appointment, but Jacob figured that Anna and Eli would talk about it later when he wasn't around.

He hoped that Bobby would be available for a chat and some gaming time when he got back to the house. He needed to spend some time with someone who really knew him.

~*~

The house had finally quieted, and Anna blew out a long breath. The day had gone well, despite still feeling like she was swimming against the tide.

After lunch at Nadine's, the day had cleared up enough for them to go for a walk. Eli had strapped Noah to his back, and then they'd taken to the trail behind the house. Anna wasn't sure she would survive a high-speed hike, but thankfully, Eli set a slow pace. Jacob walked silently behind Eli, while Anna brought up the rear. Shadow meandered out into the trees and then back again, never leaving them for long.

The only one making much noise as they walked was Noah once again as he whapped his hands on Eli's neck and head.

Anna was curious about what had happened at the doctor's office. But since neither Jacob nor Eli had volunteered anything about the visit, she knew she'd have to wait. Hopefully, they'd be able to have a conversation about the situation with Jacob later, after he'd gone up to his room.

During her time alone at the lodge earlier, she'd spent some time thinking things over and actually praying about them, which she admittedly hadn't done much of. She felt more settled and capable of having a calm discussion with Eli about everything.

Whether it was a mindset that would last, she wasn't sure. Anna just hoped that if it didn't, knowing that with some effort she could get back to that place would encourage her to keep trying.

She finished putting the last of the dishes in the dishwasher, then wiped down the counters. Eli had taken Noah upstairs to give him a bath and get him ready for bed. He had given Jacob permission to spend a few hours on the Xbox with his friend, so he'd disappeared upstairs to his room as soon as he'd helped clear the table.

Eli reappeared with Noah just as Anna finished preparing his bottle. She took Noah from Eli and settled into the rocker recliner in the living room next to the still-bare Christmas tree.

"So how did the appointment go?" she asked as Eli began to make a fire in the fireplace. "Is everything okay?"

"Yeah. Ryker said that he's fine. Just needs to eat more healthy food." Eli glanced over at her. "I also asked about a therapist for him, but I'm not sure if Jacob wants to go."

"I get that," Anna said. "I wasn't sure about going either."

Eli paused and sat back on his heels, focusing on her. "How do you feel about it now?"

She considered her answer, shifting her gaze to Noah for a moment as she ran her hand over his hair. He looked up at her with wide eyes as he continued to drink his bottle.

"It was necessary," she said. "But I can also see that it is beneficial. It kind of feels like I've been given the opportunity to grab onto a life preserver."

Eli turned his attention back to the fire. "I guess you've felt like you've been caught up in a rushing river, huh?"

"A bit." Anna realized that Eli would likely struggle with the idea that she felt like she was drowning and that he hadn't been able to save her. That it had taken a stranger to give her the life preserver she needed.

Anna hated that she'd hurt him that way. Eli took the role of caring for those he loved very seriously. If he thought that he hadn't been able to care for her well enough, he would feel like he'd failed.

"I might have needed a life preserver to get out of that rushing river, but you were my rock. You were the thing that kept me from being completely swept away. I wouldn't be here without you." Anna wished she could go to him and wrap her arms around him, and to feel his strong arms around her. "You're my rock, Eli. I love you and can't imagine how I would have survived any of this without you by my side."

Eli stared into the flickering flames, his profile not revealing the thoughts going through his head.

"I haven't been able to be there for you the way you've needed—especially recently," she said. "And I'm so sorry for that."

He turned at her words, his brow furrowed. "You have nothing to be sorry for, sweetheart. I understood that you were—you *are*—dealing with a lot, and if I could take any of that from you, I would."

Noah flung his bottle onto the floor beside Eli with a squeal. Eli scooped it up and got to his feet. "Let me take him up and see if I can get him to sleep."

"When you come back down, I think we need to talk."

Eli hesitated, then nodded. "It might be a little while."

"I'm sure it will be," she said with a little laugh.

Smiling, Eli said, "I'll be back."

After he'd left with Noah, Anna grabbed the blanket from the back of the recliner and covered her legs as she drew them up onto the chair. The only light in the room came from the fire and the lamp on one of the end tables.

In the past, the tree would have been decorated already, its lights casting a beautiful glow in the room. Hopefully, they could get the tree decorated in the next couple of days. She wondered if Jacob would like to help decorate it, or if that wasn't something the teen would be interested in.

Though she and Eli needed to actually discuss it, Anna knew that Jacob would be staying with them. If her mind and emotions hadn't been so messed up, she would have accepted that decision much sooner.

Accepting it, however, didn't do away with all her doubts about whether she could be what Jacob needed. She was quite sure that he didn't want her to be his mom, and that was understandable.

But she would need to play some sort of role in his life. If he didn't want that, then living together might be a little difficult.

The only way this would work, she realized, was if everything was on the table. Jacob needed to voice how he felt about being part of their family. They all had issues and needs that had to be taken into consideration.

Anna was still worried that her own issues would cause problems. But if she could be honest with Eli and Jacob about how she was feeling, maybe things would be okay. She knew that she'd have good days and bad days, but hopefully with the therapist's help, she wouldn't have so many bad days in a row, like she had experienced recently.

It was close to half an hour before Eli reappeared with the baby monitor in hand. He gave her a weary smile as he slumped down on the couch and set the monitor on the end table. "Mom swears that one day he'll actually fall asleep on his own. I just wish he didn't seem to hate sleep so much when it's something his body needs."

"I feel like his resistance to sleep is in direct correlation to our need for it," Anna said. "I never realized how much I relied on sleep to be able to function normally."

"Feels like a case of us not really knowing what we had until we didn't have it anymore."

Everything was changing, and she needed to accept those changes and move forward. Constantly looking back and wishing for how things used to be only made her struggle more.

"Did you check on Jacob?" she asked.

Eli nodded. "He's chatting and gaming with Bobby. Happiest I've seen him since he got here."

"I'm okay with it."

Eli stared at her for a moment, his brows drawn together. "With what?"

"With Jacob being part of our family."

"Really?" His voice was laced with skepticism, and she couldn't blame him for it. "What changed your mind?"

"I think I always knew that keeping Jacob with us was the right thing to do." She stared into the fire for a moment. "My struggle was with feeling that if I couldn't give Jacob what he needed, I would fail yet one more person."

"And you don't feel that way anymore?"

"Oh, never fear. I still feel that way," she said with a brief laugh. "But it isn't really fair to punish Jacob for my own fear of failing. Plus, I'm not on my own, so even if I do fail him, you'll be there to help."

"Sweetheart, I know I've told you before, but I'm going to say it again: you haven't failed anyone. We're all fine."

She knew that Eli meant well, but he just would never understand. He'd never struggled with feeling like he needed to be perfect. His struggles early in his life had made him strong and steady. What she'd dealt with recently was all new to her, and clearly, she didn't know how to cope the way he did.

"One thing I want to make sure of is that we communicate," Anna said, reiterating what the therapist had said to her. "All of us. I think that will give us the best chance of succeeding."

Eli nodded. "Maybe the three of us should go to therapy."

Anna thought that was a good idea. Anything that would give them a fighting chance at making this next chapter of their lives successful. They talked for a bit more about how they would move forward with Jacob as part of their family, focusing on his most immediate needs like new clothes for school.

"One thing I think you need to consider is telling him the truth," Anna said.

"Really?" Eli frowned. "How am I supposed to do that? Just say, *Oh, by the way, your mom got pregnant with you when she was raped, so I'm not really your dad?*"

"I guess that's something a therapist could help us with. But yes, I think he needs to know the truth. If we don't tell him, it might end up accidentally coming out later, and then what?"

"Is he old enough to understand, though?"

"I think he is," Anna said. "I mean, he's dealt with his mom's mental illness. And maybe that information might help him understand better what she went through."

Eli rubbed the back of his neck. "My inclination is to protect him, you know?"

"I guess we should make an appointment with the therapist Ryker recommended first, then move forward with her guidance and a lot of prayer. If she says wait, then we definitely wait." Anna got out of the recliner and went to where Eli sat. He opened his arms, and she settled on his lap. "I know it seemed like I didn't want him here, but it was just too much all at once, you know? We can do this together."

"I want what's best for all of us." Eli wrapped his arms around her, pulling her close. "I love you so much."

"I can't promise I'm always going to handle everything the way I should," she told him as she looped her arms around his neck. "But I'm going to try harder than I have been."

"Just remember that you're not alone," Eli reminded her. "This won't work for any of us if you insist on doing it all yourself. Now, more than ever, we're going to need the help and support of our family."

"I'll try to remember that, but sometimes there's a voice in my head that tells me that I *should* be able to do it all myself."

"I'm going to call you on it, if I see you trying to do that," he said.

"Thank you." She cupped his face in her hands and pressed her lips to his, then whispered, "Thank you for loving me enough to do that."

"Always."

Something settled inside her then, and a feeling of rightness filled her. The peace she felt about all of it could only have come from God.

It should have been this way for the last several months. The two of them being there to support each other. Somewhere along the way, she'd lost sight of that. She knew she wasn't out of the storm just yet, but she clung to Eli's promise that he would remind her that she wasn't alone when those moments came, when she got lost in the doubts and fears in her mind.

CHAPTER SEVENTEEN

Jacob punched the air in silent victory, mindful of the fact that Eli was trying to put Noah to bed just down the hallway. It was good that he was already used to playing games quietly, since Bobby's mom had always told them to not be loud. He wouldn't risk being too loud regardless, because he didn't want to chance having his Xbox taken away if he woke the baby.

"How's it going?"

Seeing Eli in the door of his room, Jacob reached up and pushed his headset off. "It's going good. We just got a Victory Royale."

"And that is?" Eli asked.

Sometimes Jacob forgot that not every guy was as interested in video games as he and Bobby were. "We were the last team left at the end of game."

"Nice. Sounds like you and Bobby did well."

Jacob nodded. "Bobby actually made it to the end this time too, which he usually doesn't."

A smile crossed Eli's face. "Well, have fun."

"I will. Thanks for letting me play with Bobby tonight."

"You're welcome."

As Jacob watched Eli close the door, he was surprised the man hadn't given him a specific bedtime. Being able to play unlimited games with Bobby and chat with his friend felt great. In fact, it was the best he'd felt since coming to New Hope.

However, he knew it wouldn't last because whether he liked it or not, he was going to have to go to school. Plus, his experience with his mom had taught him that those great moments never

A LOVE TO SHARE · 143

lasted. They were like little blips that came and went far too quickly.

"Ready up, man," Bobby said, pulling his thoughts back to the moment.

Pressing the button on his controller, he said, "I'm ready."

They played another game, but this time, when it came down to just them and one other team, they were the ones eliminated.

"I'm gonna get more chips," Bobby said. "I'll be right back."

"I'm going to grab a drink."

Jacob set his controller down and put his headset on the bed. He left his room and walked quietly past Noah's room to the stairs. As he went down the stairs, he could hear the murmur of conversation. He paused, uncertain if he should keep going because he didn't want to interrupt Anna and Eli if they were talking.

Before he could decide, Anna's voice rose to a level that Jacob could clearly hear.

"He needs to know the truth, though."

Jacob gripped the railing. Were they talking about him?

"Really? How am I supposed to do that? Just say, *Oh, by the way, your mom got pregnant with you when she was raped, so I'm not really your dad?*"

Jacob's heart began to race, the blood pounding in his ears muffling all other sounds. He turned and gripped the rail with both hands, afraid his knees were going to give out and send him crashing down the stairs.

His mom had been...? Jacob couldn't even think the word. He didn't want to even imagine that his father had *attacked* his mom. But... why would Eli say that if it wasn't true?

He needed to get back to his room, but his body was frozen. Digging deep, Jacob forced himself to turn and, as quietly as possible, he climbed the steps back to the second floor. He made it to his room and grabbed his headset before going into his bathroom and locking the door.

"Bobby?" he gasped. "Bobby, are you there?"

"Yeah. What's up?"

Tears stung Jacob's eyes, and he took several gulping breaths, trying not to let out the sobs that wanted to break free.

"Jake? What's wrong?"

"I just heard..." Jacob paused and struggled to take a deep breath, his shoulders lifting with the moment. "I just heard Eli say that he's not my real dad."

"What? Why would he say that?" Bobby asked. "That's crazy."

Jacob's heart hurt so badly. For himself, but more for his mom. What he had just heard explained so much, not the least of which was how she'd been able to leave him. She'd probably hated knowing that his biological fath...—he couldn't even call him that—his biological donor had attacked her in such a horrible way.

"Bobby, my mom got pregnant with me when she was *raped*."

"Whoa. Really, dude?"

"That's what Eli said to Anna." Jacob huddled down against the door, his whole body shaking with the shock of the revelation. "My mom must have told him, even though my birth certificate said Eli was my dad."

"What are you going to do?"

Jacob pressed his forehead to his knees. "I don't know." The words came as a whisper. "I don't know. They're not going to want me to stay here if I'm not Eli's kid."

"Then why did he come get you? Why is he letting you stay with him?"

Jacob didn't know the answers to those questions, but he was pretty sure that they were trying to figure out somewhere else for him to go. But where would that be? He hadn't even met his grandfather yet, and his aunt couldn't take him since she lived where she worked.

Fear gripped him at the thought of being sent to yet another home. "Would your mom let me live with you? If I could get back there, maybe she would let me stay?"

"She might," Bobby said, and he actually sounded as if he really thought she would. "But how're you gonna get back here? Do you have any money?"

"I have some that Mom left for me." But it might not be enough. Despair filled him. Maybe if he told Rhett he could return all the stuff, he might give him the money instead. Then he could buy a plane ticket.

But he didn't know how to get hold of Rhett, and he had no phone to call anyone. All he knew right then was that he needed to go. Leave before they sent him away.

"I'm gonna try and get there. But don't tell your mom, okay?"

"I dunno, Jake. You think you should do this by yourself?"

Jacob had no options. He had no one but himself.

With determination, Jacob pushed aside the revelations of the night and got to his feet. He leaned against the bathroom door, waiting for his legs to stop trembling. He needed to get control of his body before he could do anything else.

When he finally felt steadier, he went back into the bedroom and straight to the closet where he'd put his suitcase and backpack. He couldn't take the suitcase, so he had to use the space in his backpack carefully.

He'd wear a pair of jeans, a long-sleeve shirt, and a hoodie, so he put in a few pairs of underwear and socks as well as his favorite T-shirts. There was no way he'd leave his sketch book behind. He wasn't a talented artist or anything, but the book contained little sketches he and his mom had done for each other. She'd also used it to leave him messages, so he had to take it with him.

After a brief pause, he put the tablet in the backpack as well. Jacob hoped Rhett wouldn't be mad, but if he could find places with Wi-Fi along the way, he could hopefully keep in contact with Bobby.

If need be, he could mail it back to Rhett once he got back to Bobby's.

"What are you going to do?" Bobby asked again. "I think I should tell my mom."

"If you do that, and she says no, I won't have anywhere else to go." Jacob slumped down on the edge of the bed, his backpack beside him. "I miss my mom so much. If she'd just stayed, I wouldn't have to do this."

"I know, man." Bobby's voice was soft, and Jacob knew it was because he truly did understand how much Jacob missed his mom.

He and Bobby had known each other for years, and in that time, Bobby had witnessed the ups and downs he'd had with his mom. He also knew how much Jacob had loved her since she was his only parent. Bobby had a dad, but he hardly ever saw him, so he was close with his mom, too.

"I can't stay here, and I don't know where else to go." Bobby's apartment had been like a second home for many years, and now Jacob hoped it would be the place where he'd finally feel like he belonged.

"But what if you get here and my mom says no?"

Jacob hoped she wouldn't do that if he was already on her doorstep. She'd always been kind to him, treating him like a second son.

"It's a chance I've gotta take."

"I hope she says yes," Bobby said. "It would be great to have you here again. School sucks without you."

"I haven't gone to school here yet. But if I stay, I'm sure I have to start soon."

He got back up and looked around the room, making sure that he wasn't leaving anything that was important to him. Aside from all the electronics, he hadn't gotten anything else new.

Finally, he went to the chest of drawers and pulled open the bottom drawer. Inside it was the packet of pictures of him and his mom, along with cards she'd given him over the years. She'd kept it all for him, maybe in anticipation of losing the battle she fought every day with her mental illness.

Clutching it in his hand, he took it to his backpack and slid it inside. He still had some books and more clothes, but there was no way he could take them. Maybe, once he was settled with Bobby and his mom, Eli would be willing to send the stuff to him.

"When are you going to leave?"

"I want to leave *now*, but I'll have to wait until they're asleep."

"They don't have a house alarm?"

"Nope. I haven't seen anything like that."

"Are you going to hitchhike or something?"

"I'm not sure." Jacob pulled the tablet out again and opened up the map app. He typed in the name of the lodge and then put in the destination of New Hope Falls. "I think I'll walk to town. I should be able to do that in a couple of hours."

"And then what?"

He really wasn't sure, but he hoped that as he went, he'd figure things out. There was no doubt he was scared. What he was doing wasn't safe, but he hoped that it would pay off in the end.

"I'll figure something out," he murmured as he studied the map. He wondered if he could find a flashlight because he wasn't sure there would be streetlights along the rural road leading from the lodge to the town. "Let's play some more. I can't leave for a while."

He took screenshots of the maps of New Hope and the road leading from the lodge to the town, then plugged the tablet in so it would be fully charged when he left. He set his backpack on the floor on the far side of the bed, then sat back down in front of the television and picked up the controller.

"Okay. Let's ready up."

They played several more games, with Jacob being the one to be eliminated first in each one. His mind was just not on video games, but he needed to kill time until Anna and Eli had gone to sleep.

"You know what your mom would say about what you're planning?" Bobby asked after their team was eliminated early in yet another game.

Jacob knew exactly what she'd say. *I'm not calling you stupid, but this idea of yours sure is.* She'd be right, but what else could he do? He didn't want people to force him to move yet again, to be with more strangers. He knew that there was no way for his mom to come back, but maybe he could get some of his old life back. His friend. His school—such as it was. He just wanted it all back, and this was the only way he knew to get it.

"I still don't know how you're going to do this without lots of money. How're you going to eat?"

"I'll take some granola bars and stuff from here. They said I could eat what I want."

It was getting close to eleven, but he didn't know exactly what time Anna and Eli went to bed. Maybe he should get a drink, like he'd planned to originally and see if they were still awake.

"I'll be back," he told Bobby, then took off his headset and set it down with his controller. If they had gone to bed, he'd use this as a trial run to see if they'd come out while he was in the kitchen getting something to drink.

The hallway was dark except for the small pools of light cast by the nightlights that were plugged into sockets along the wall. The stairs weren't as well lit, so he grabbed the rail to guide him down to the main floor.

It was dark there as well except for more nightlights, so Anna and Eli had gone to bed. He didn't keep his movements too stealthy as he made his way to the kitchen. There was a nightlight on the wall above the counter, and it gave enough light for him to open the fridge and grab a bottle of water.

He also opened the cupboard where Anna had said he could get snacks if he was hungry. Without checking to see what was there, he grabbed a handful of granola bars, then tucked the water bottle under his arm and snagged an apple from the bowl on the counter.

Back up in his room, he dropped all of it on his bed, then put his headset back on. "You still here?"

"Yep. Ready to play again?"

"Just a second." Jacob grabbed his backpack and put the food and water in it. He would grab a bit more before he left, just so he had stuff to eat and drink on the way since he couldn't afford to buy food if he wanted to have enough money for a ticket.

"I should probably go. Everything is quiet downstairs."

"Jake, I'm worried. I don't think this is a good idea."

Jacob was worried too, but he was also desperate. What had made his mom think that Eli would want him when he wasn't his kid? He seemed like a decent enough guy. But even so, he had a wife now and a kid of his own. Why would he want some other guy's kid? A guy who was a rapist?

The very idea that he had the genes of a man who could do something like that made Jacob want to throw up. How was he supposed to deal with that knowledge?

Eli probably didn't want to have someone like him around his own kid, but he was too nice to just dump him off on someone else. Yet. That moment was sure to come though, and Jacob didn't want to be around for it.

"It'll be fine."

"Find Wi-Fi as often as you can so that you can let me know how you're doing."

"I will, but I gotta go now."

"Be careful, man."

Jacob's stomach clenched with worry, but he tried to ignore it. "I'll see you soon."

"I can't wait."

He said goodbye, then sat on the edge of the bed, clutching the controller in his hand. He wouldn't have to be dealing with any of this if his mom had just stayed with him. Or if she'd made arrangements for him to stay with Bobby and his mom.

Tears pricked his eyes as he thought of her again, missing her so intensely that the pain felt like an actual wound in his chest. Taking a deep breath, he got to his feet and prepared to leave. He put on a couple of shirts under his hoodie, just in case it was colder than he realized, and he doubled up on his socks as well.

Once he was ready, he sneaked down the stairs, making another quick stop in the kitchen to get water and more food. Then he approached the door. Movement had him jumping until he realized it was Shadow.

"Goodbye, boy." He whispered the words as he ruffled the dog's fur. When he opened the door, Shadow didn't try to go out with him, which was good because Jacob wasn't sure how he'd deal with that situation.

As he closed the door and headed down the steps, Jacob glanced up at the sky. He was glad to see that the moon was nearly full, so as long as it didn't get cloudy, it shouldn't be too dark for him to find his way to town. Unfortunately, it was chillier than he'd expected, and he wished he had put on a few more layers. He wasn't going to go back inside, though, so he'd just have to hope he'd warm up as he walked.

It didn't take too long to get to the entrance of the property, where he turned toward the town, trying to quell his nerves at being alone on a deserted rural road. If he heard any cars coming, he'd just duck into the trees until they passed. He wouldn't accept any rides just yet. If he could get to a bus station, he would hopefully have enough money to buy tickets to make it all the way to Shreve-port.

As he began his solitary walk, alone except for his thoughts, it was hard not to focus on his grief. The longing to have a place to belong, somewhere in the world, felt like something he'd never have. For a while, he'd thought maybe it was a possibility. But knowing what he did about himself now, Jacob was positive there was no place where he'd truly ever belong.

He tipped his head back and stared at the dark sky. What was the sense of living if it was all just so hopeless? As the question clouded his thoughts, he realized that that was probably something his mom had wondered as well.

CHAPTER EIGHTEEN

The buzzing of his phone jerked Kieran Sutherland from sleep. Instantly awake, he grabbed it off the nightstand and flipped the blankets off to get out of bed, hopefully without waking Cara. As he walked to the bedroom door, he hit the button to answer it but didn't say anything until he was in the hallway.

"What's up?"

"Hey, Chief. Sorry to bother you so late, but I've got a situation here."

With the phone pressed to his ear, Kieran headed toward the kitchen. "What sort of situation?"

"I was driving around, and I saw a kid walking with a backpack on. I stopped to chat with him, and I think maybe you should come in and talk to him."

"Is he a local?"

"That's what I'm not sure about," the officer said.

"Did he give you his name?" Kieran ran a hand through his hair. It was unusual for one of his guys to call him in the middle of the night unless it was a real emergency. A runaway kid, though unusual, wasn't that much of an emergency.

"Yeah. Said it was Jacob McNamara."

Kieran froze. "McNamara?"

"Yeah. That's why I called."

"I'll be there in ten." Kieran ended the call and went to the spare bedroom where he kept some clothes just in case something like this happened.

He pulled on a pair of jeans and a T-shirt, thinking he'd keep it casual when talking to the kid. As he dressed, he tried to figure out why the boy he was pretty sure was Sheila's son who'd come to live with Eli was wandering around New Hope at two o'clock in the morning. There didn't seem to be a good reason, which was concerning, to say the least.

As he drove to the station, he prayed for wisdom in dealing with a situation that was clearly troubling. He let himself into the station, then made his way to his office. It was dark, so he headed for the next likely place they'd be.

Sure enough, his officer was in the break room with the kid. He glanced up, relief crossing his face when he saw Kieran.

"Hey, chief."

Kieran nodded at the man. "Thanks for calling me. I've got this now."

The officer took his words for the dismissal they were and left the room. Kieran turned his attention to the boy who sat at the table, his gaze on the can of soda and bag of chips in front of him.

"Hi there," he said. "I'm Kieran."

He held out his hand. The boy looked up, then shook it without hesitation. "Jacob."

Kieran sat down across the table and gave him a smile. "So, what brings you out so late at night?"

"I'm going to the bus station."

"Where you headed?" he asked.

The boy's brow furrowed for a moment. "Shreveport."

"Louisiana?" Jacob nodded. "What's in Shreveport?"

Jacob didn't answer right away, his gaze focused again on the bag of chips in front of him. "It's where I used to live with my mom."

Kieran was aware of what had happened to Sheila, so he didn't ask about her. Already, the boy looked like he carried the weight of the world on his shoulders. What had gone so wrong at Eli and Anna's that he'd struck out on his own, determined to cross the country alone, back to where he'd used to live, even though his mom was no longer there?

"And you want to live there? Not here in New Hope?"

The teen's shoulders slumped, and he fiddled with the chip bag. "Yeah."

"I'm sure it's hard to move from where you've lived to some-place new. Sometimes it just takes time to adjust."

Jacob shook his head. "I don't belong here."

"But your dad and your aunt are here."

He looked up then, realization on his face that Kieran knew who he was. "He's not my dad."

"What?"

"He's not my dad, and there's no place here for me." Jacob paused. "I can't live with my grandpa or my aunt, and Eli isn't my dad."

"Why would you say that?"

"Because it's true. I heard him and Anna talking. She said he needed to tell me the truth, which is that he's not my dad and that my real dad is a rapist." Jacob cleared his throat, then bit his lip. "They don't want me here. I need to go back."

Kieran's heart ached for the teen. He was so young to have to deal with such weighty issues in his life, and Kieran couldn't blame him at all for wanting to return to what was familiar. "Are you going back to someone in particular?"

Jacob nodded. "My best friend, Bobby. We're hoping that his mom will let me live with them. He doesn't care who my dad is. He just wants to be my friend." Jacob swallowed hard. "I miss him."

"I think Eli would actually be upset if you left like this," Kieran said.

"Why would he? This way, he doesn't have to have someone like me around his family."

"Someone like you?"

"Yeah. You know. A kid whose mom killed herself and who has a rapist for a father."

Kieran knew he couldn't keep speaking for Eli. He had no idea what the man planned to do about Jacob. Maybe taking responsibility for a child who wasn't biologically his was too much to ask. He wouldn't have thought so, but Kieran also knew that Eli had other things to consider, what with having a baby in their family now.

"Did Eli say that?"

Jacob shrugged. "He didn't have to. They don't want me as part of the family, plus I think Anna is having some issues herself. They have their family with Noah, and I'm not part of that."

Kieran found himself at a loss as to what to say. "I think you need to have a conversation with the adults involved in this. That means Eli, Anna, Josie, and Bobby's mom. Tell them how you're feeling."

Jacob shook his head, his thin face pinched with grief. "I already know there's no place for me here. I don't want to hear them say it."

"You can't make these decisions on your own, I'm afraid."

"I just want a place to belong," he said, his voice wavering. The chip bag crinkled in his hands. "I want to be with people who want me around. I don't expect people to love me. Even my mom didn't love me enough to stay. But I just... want someplace..."

The emotions that gripped Jacob wound their way around Kieran's heart. And more than anything, he wanted to assure Jacob that there was a place for him in the world. However, he knew that the words from him would mean nothing. Absolutely nothing. Jacob didn't know him, so nothing he said would make a difference to the teen.

"I need to call Eli and let him know you're here."

"Please. No," Jacob pleaded. "Can't you just let me go? Pretend you never saw me?"

"It's not safe for you to travel on your own like this," Kieran said. "If Bobby's mom agrees to let you live with them, and Eli is okay with it, they'll make sure that you get there safely."

"I just don't want to hear him say it. I know he's not really my dad, but I don't want to hear him say that he doesn't want me and that he's okay with me leaving. I just want to... leave."

"I know you might not feel it right now, but there are people who care about you here."

Jacob gave a shake of his head. "I don't think so."

"Josie cares about you." Kieran was confident about that. "And I think she'd be sad if you left."

"But I can't live with her. She doesn't have her own place."

"Would you rather I call her?"

Jacob laid his head on his arms on the table, an air of defeat engulfing him. "Do whatever. No one cares what I want." He sniffled. "I just want my mom."

Kieran wasn't given to tears, but the despair in the boy's voice and words made his eyes sting. He didn't know what to do, but in his heart, he felt like he needed to call Eli. If for no other reason than to let him know where Jacob was. He might not realize he was missing yet, but he would in a few hours.

"If you promise not to run again, you can come home with me and sleep there. We'll deal with everything in the morning."

Jacob looked up at him, his eyes shining with moisture. He let out a long, resigned sigh, then nodded. "You're still gonna call Eli?"

"I have to. He's the one responsible for you, so he needs to know what's going on."

"He's not gonna care. Even when he was supposed to be my dad, he never told me I could call him that. He never told me what to call him."

Kieran felt for the boy in front of him, but he also felt for his friend, who was dealing with a situation he'd probably never imagined he'd ever face.

Leaning forward, Kieran reached across the table to rest his hand on Jacob's shoulder. "We'll get this all sorted out, okay? But for now, let's head to my house and get some sleep."

Jacob nodded and pushed his chair back. Bending over, he picked up a backpack that appeared to be stuffed to the brim. Once he'd slung it onto his back and up onto his narrow shoulders, Kieran led the way out of the break room.

"We're off," Kieran said to the officer who sat at his desk.

The man got to his feet. "Do I need to do anything about this?"

"Nope. I'll take care of it."

They said goodnight, then walked out into the chilly night air. "Did you walk all the way from the lodge?"

"Yeah. Took longer than I thought, though."

Kieran unlocked the car, and soon, they were on their way back to the house he and Cara were renting. They'd lived in Cara's apartment following their wedding. But when Cara had gotten pregnant, they'd realized they needed more space. There hadn't been anything for sale that they liked, so they were just renting for the time being, waiting until they found a suitable house to buy.

Jacob quietly followed him into the house, pausing just inside the door. Kieran showed him where to leave his shoes and jacket, then took him to the room that was set up with a daybed. After he got the teen settled, Kieran debated going back to bed, but he didn't want to wake Cara. He also wasn't totally convinced that Jacob wouldn't try to sneak out.

With that in mind, he settled into his favorite recliner, knowing he could sleep almost as well there as he did in their bed. The bassinet next to the recliner was currently empty, but there'd been plenty of times when Kieran had dozed there while Jayden slept in it.

That night, sleep didn't come quickly, so he spent time praying for wisdom as he tried to help Eli and Jacob figure out their situation. He had no idea what the end result should be, but he knew that God saw the need for a decision to be made, and hopefully, He'd guide them to the right one.

~*~

Eli heard Noah begin to fuss and quickly turned the monitor down. Moving quietly, he got out of bed, glancing at the clock as he got to his feet. Three o'clock. Noah had slept a pretty solid stretch since nine, so Eli tried to be happy about that. But honestly, he'd really like to have one whole night of sleep.

He climbed the stairs to the second floor and went to Noah's crib. He was sitting up and fussing more loudly. Without saying anything, Eli tried to get him to lie down again, but that only led to him getting more upset.

Finally, he lifted him out of the crib, then went to sit in the rocker recliner they'd purchased for the room when they'd figured out how little he liked to sleep. Both he and Anna had spent a lot of time sitting in the chair with Noah over the past few months.

Eli sat down in the chair, settling the baby in the crook of his arm with his favorite blanket in his hand. He began to gently rock the chair but didn't interact with Noah verbally.

It took almost half an hour before he was sound asleep enough to transfer him back to the crib. As always, he waited to see if he would wake back up again. When he didn't, Eli stepped out of the room and pulled the door closed behind him.

As he stepped into the hallway, he glanced at Jacob's door. He wondered what time the teen had finally gone to sleep. Given that Bobby was in a time zone two hours ahead of them, it was unlikely that he had stayed up too late.

Grasping the doorknob, Eli opened the door and peered inside. He'd expected the illumination from the nightlight in the room to show him a lump in the bed. Instead, all he saw was the bed covered with the comforter, like it had been when he'd talked with Jacob earlier.

Puzzled, Eli walked into the room and flicked on the light switch. A glance across the room showed him that the bathroom door was open, but the light was off. Where was Jacob?

He looked around the room, dread filling him. After a moment's hesitation, he went to the closet and opened it. The suitcase he'd arrived with sat there, but his backpack was gone. There were still clothes in the chest of drawers, but Eli had no way of knowing if some might be missing.

Turning, he left the room and went back downstairs. The lights were all off, so he turned them on in order to look around. Where had he gone?

Still wearing his flannel pajama pants and long sleeve T-shirt, he pulled on his shoes and grabbed a jacket from the front closet, along with his keys. Though it didn't make any sense, he'd check to see if Jacob was in any of the cabins or the lodge before he raised the alarm.

If he truly had run away, where would he have gone? And *why* would he run away? The only thing Eli hadn't been able to give him was Bobby. Was he on his way to him?

The very idea made Eli feel sick. There was no way it was safe for Jacob to travel all the way to Shreveport on his own.

He climbed into the SUV and drove to the first cabin. It was locked, as were each of the other ones. He didn't bother to check the lodge. If Jacob had really run away, it was more likely that he was on the road than in the lodge.

Turning onto the road that led toward New Hope, Eli prayed that wherever Jacob was, that he was safe. So much harm could come to a boy of his age, especially since he looked younger than he really was.

Eli drove slowly, wishing he had a way of searching the sides of the road. When he reached New Hope with no sign of Jacob, Eli knew he needed help if he was going to find Jacob before something bad happened to him. If it hadn't already.

Stopping at the side of the street, Eli pulled out his phone. As he did, he realized that he'd forgotten to return the monitor to the bedroom, so Anna wouldn't hear Noah if he woke up. He tapped the screen to call her, knowing she needed to know what was going on anyway.

"Eli?" She still sounded half asleep. "Why are you calling me?"

"I think Jacob's run away."

"What?"

"I checked his room when I got up with Noah a bit ago, and he wasn't there, and his bed wasn't slept in. I'm going to call Kieran and see if he can help look for him. I wanted you to know what was going on, plus I didn't put the monitor back in the room after I settled Noah."

"Why would he run away?"

"I don't know, but I'm scared for him."

"I am too," Anna said. "Go ahead and call Kieran, then call me back after you've talked to him."

"I'm sorry to have to wake you like this."

"Don't worry about that. Finding Jacob is more important than anything else right now. I'll be praying that God keeps him safe and that you find him quickly."

"Thanks, sweetheart. I love you."

"I love you too."

As soon as he hung up with her, he brought up Kieran's contact info and tapped the screen to call him, worrying only for a moment about waking the man up in the middle of the night.

"He's safe, Eli," Kieran said when he answered.

"What?"

"My officer found Jacob on the street earlier. I brought him home with me because I didn't think you'd notice he was missing until the morning."

Relief flooded Eli, and he let out a loud sigh. "I was so worried."

"I'm sorry, man. He wasn't keen to go back to your place just yet, so I offered to let him sleep here. I planned to give you call at a more respectable hour to let you know he was here."

"Why did he run away?"

Kieran didn't answer right away, and when he did, it wasn't with an actual answer. "He's dealing with a lot."

"I understand that," Eli said. "The way Sheila died has probably been difficult for him to accept, along with having to move away from his best friend."

"And also hearing that you're not his real dad and that he's the son of a rapist."

Kieran's words were like a punch to the gut. "He heard us?"

"Yes, and now he's convinced that you don't want him. That no one ever will."

CHAPTER NINETEEN

Eli took a deep, shuddering breath. How much more could he mess up? The thought of what could have happened to Jacob made him sick. He should have known not to talk about those topics in a place where Jacob might overhear them. He'd just figured Jacob was focused on his video games, so he wouldn't hear their conversation.

"Go on home, Eli," Kieran said. "I'll bring Jacob there in a few hours. We'll get this all sorted out."

"Thanks." Eli would have preferred to tackle the problem right away, but he was going to trust Kieran. Trust that his friend, who was also the police chief, knew what he was doing.

"I'll see you in a few hours."

After the call ended, Eli gripped the steering wheel, watching as drizzling rain blurred the streetlamps into weeping blobs of light. He needed to call Anna back and let her know Jacob was safe. He needed to go home.

But for a few moments, he also needed to just sit in silence by himself. He loosened his grip on the steering wheel and rubbed his hands over his face, not surprised to find wetness on his cheeks. In that moment, he understood how Anna could feel like she was a failure when things weren't going right.

Except, in his situation, he really *had* failed Jacob. There was no way to hide the ramifications of his failure with the teen. If Jacob had felt like the only option was to run away in the middle of the night, Eli had definitely failed.

Please, God, help Jacob. Let him know that even though I've failed him, he isn't alone. And give me wisdom to know what to do... what's best for Jacob.

He'd thought he'd figured out what that was after he and Anna had talked, but now, he had no idea what Jacob might want.

Knowing that Anna would be worried, he picked up his phone and tapped the screen to call her. The panic he'd felt had drained away with the news that Jacob was okay, but it had left behind a bone-deep weariness mixed with grief over the pain he'd caused Jacob.

"Did you find him?" Anna asked instead of a greeting.

"Well, I didn't find him. One of Kieran's officers picked him up and took him to the station, then called Kieran."

"Why didn't Kieran call us?"

"He said that he didn't think we'd notice he was missing until morning, so he took him home to his place for the night."

"Did he say why he ran away?"

Eli sighed. "He heard us talking about me not being his dad and who his real dad was."

"Oh." Anna's voice was soft. "That's not how he should have found out."

"I know. I just didn't think he'd hear us."

"What do we do now?"

"We wait until morning, then we talk to Jacob." Eli sighed. "I wish we had a professional to help us with this. I'm afraid I'm going to say the wrong thing."

"We won't have time to call anyone before we talk to him, though, right?"

"Yeah." Eli dragged a hand through his hair. "I'll just be honest with him and ask him to give us a few days to figure things out. In that time, hopefully we'll be able to speak with someone who could help."

"What will you do if he doesn't want to stay with us?" Anna asked.

"I don't know. I guess we cross that bridge when we get to it."

"Come home, darling. Let's get some rest now that we know Jacob is safe."

"Alright. I'll be there in a few minutes."

"Drive safe."

"I will." Eli ended the call and dropped his phone into the cup holder, then started up the SUV to make the drive back to the house.

It was unreal how Sheila had still managed to complicate his life, even without being there in person. He didn't wish that she hadn't listed him on Jacob's birth certificate, but it would have helped this current situation if she'd just been upfront with her son about what had happened. Instead, she'd left it to Eli to break that news to him, all the while letting Jacob think Eli was his dad.

Back at the house, he crawled into bed with Anna and wrapped his arms around her.

"I think everything will work out," she said as she held him tightly. "I know I haven't been the most supportive of Jacob being here, and I'm sorry about that."

"It wasn't something either of us could have prepared for. I just want to do what's right for Jacob, and if that means he stays with us, then I want that. If it means he goes somewhere else, I'll do my best to make that happen for him."

With their foreheads pressed together, they spent some time in whispered prayer, then as they settled into silence, Eli tried his best to fall asleep. Unfortunately, his thoughts weren't inclined to let that happen.

He did eventually fall asleep, but it wasn't for long. Noah woke them both a little after seven. Though Anna got up with him, Eli knew he couldn't fall back asleep, so he crawled out of bed as well.

Kieran called him around eight to see if it was a good time to bring Jacob home. Eli told him it was since both he and Anna were up and dressed. He was already on his second cup of coffee.

He and Anna prayed again as they waited for Kieran and Jacob to arrive. No doubt Jacob was worried about the reception he'd get, so Eli prayed specifically for peace for the teen.

Anna had prepared some cinnamon rolls and cut up some strawberries, which Jacob had enjoyed during his time with them. Eli's appetite was non-existent, and he was fairly sure that would be true for Jacob as well, but he hoped that perhaps once they'd had a chance to talk, that would change for both of them.

He'd planned for them to go to church that morning, but he doubted that would happen now. He hoped that now that Anna had a plan of action in place for herself, they'd be able to get back to more regular attendance. However, it didn't look like getting back to church would start that day.

When he heard the rumble of an engine approaching the house, Eli took a deep breath and blew it out. *Please, God, guide this meeting.*

He opened the door and watched as Kieran parked. The passenger side door was slow opening, but Kieran was out of the vehicle more quickly. When the teen made an appearance, his head was bent, and his shoulders slumped. He clutched his backpack and shuffled up the steps behind Kieran.

"Good morning, Eli," Kieran said, holding out his hand as he approached the door.

Eli shook his hand. "Morning. Thanks for bringing Jacob home."

"Is it okay if I hang around?" Kieran asked.

"That's fine," Eli said as he stepped back to let them into the house. "Would you like a cup of coffee?"

"I'd love one. Thanks."

As Jacob walked past him, he kept his head bent. Eli placed his hand on Jacob's shoulder and waited for the teen to look up at him. When he finally did, Eli said, "We'll get this sorted out. Everything is going to be fine. Okay?" The wariness in Jacob's gaze eased a bit at his words. "Why don't you take your backpack up to your room, then come back down for some breakfast?"

Jacob nodded and headed for the stairs. Eli watched him go, then turned to where Kieran stood with a cup of coffee in his hands.

"How do we deal with this?" Eli asked, keeping his voice low.

"I think you need to be honest with Jacob about where you see him fitting into your lives—if you do—and also be open to hearing what he might want."

Eli nodded. "I'll admit we haven't handled all of this very well. The call informing us of Sheila's passing and wishes for Jacob came at a time when we were also dealing with some other things."

"But we've got that under control now," Anna said. "Or maybe I should say that we're headed in the right direction."

Kieran glanced between the two of them. "Everything's okay?"

Eli didn't say anything since it was more Anna's story than his. Who she told the details to about what was going on was her call, not his.

Anna sighed. "I thought I was just tired since Noah apparently didn't get the memo that babies are supposed to sleep lots. Unfortunately, I'm dealing with some postpartum depression, compounded by some issues of my own making. Basically, a perfect storm that led to a bad place for me."

"But you're doing better?" Kieran's concern was clear on his face.

"I can't say that I'm doing a whole lot better yet," she said with a shrug. "But being aware of what's been happening and having a plan of action is half the battle."

"Have you talked to Cara about this?" Kieran asked.

"No." Anna frowned. "I really felt like I was failing at things, you know? And if there's one thing I don't like to admit, it's that I don't have a perfect handle on everything."

"Having a baby is no joke," Kieran said. "There are days Cara hands me Jayden the minute I walk in the door from work, just so she can take a shower. And thank goodness that my mom loves to cook. She's been making us meals regularly, and she'll come over to watch Jayden so Cara can nap if we've had a rough night with him. I think her support is the only reason we haven't lost our minds."

"I haven't been as smart as Cara," Anna said. "I felt like I needed to do it all by myself or else I wasn't doing it right."

Before she could add anything more, Jacob shuffled back into the dining room, his head bent once again.

"Hey, Noah. Look who's here," Anna said. "Want to say hi to Jacob?"

Noah let out a screech, and Jacob lifted his head. A quick smile crossed his face as he looked at Noah.

"Why don't we have some breakfast?" Eli said.

It didn't take too long to get the cinnamon rolls and fruit set out on the table, as well as hot chocolate for Jacob.

After Eli said a prayer for the meal, Jacob murmured, "I'm sorry."

"You're not in trouble, Jacob," Eli said. "I'm just sorry that you got to the point where you felt that running away was your only option. We should have talked more to you about what was going on."

"Where were you going?" Anna asked.

"I... uh... I was trying to get back to Shreveport. To Bobby's."

"I know you heard Anna and I discussing me not being your real dad and the circumstances around who your biological father is."

Jacob nodded, his gaze dropping to his plate.

"Did you think that I was surprised by the news that you weren't my son?"

He looked up and shrugged. "I didn't think you'd have let me come if you knew."

"That's not true," Eli said. "I knew the moment I received the call from the social worker that you weren't mine."

When Jacob looked up at him, his brow furrowed. "You knew before we even met?"

"Yes. I knew I wasn't your biological dad right from the start because your mom and I had never had a physical relationship when we dated."

"Really? But you still came to get me."

Eli nodded. "From the moment I heard about you, I just felt in my heart that I needed to bring you here. So that's what I did."

"It's mainly my fault that we didn't talk to you more about what we were thinking," Anna said. "I've been struggling, so Eli had to split his focus between me and Noah and you. That meant that we didn't do a good job handling things with you."

"We want you to be part of our family, Jacob," Eli said. "I'm sorry we didn't make that clear sooner."

Jacob's brow furrowed. "You want me to stay here?"

"Yes."

"Even though you're not really my dad?"

"You don't need to be biologically related to us in order to be part of our family. If you would like to stay here with us, we would be happy to call you our son."

"Even though my real dad is a... a rapist?"

"Just because he did what he did doesn't mean that you'll be the same," Eli said. "Regardless of your genetic makeup, you still have choices in life. Your biological father had a choice, and he made the wrong one. It is my prayer that when you're presented with choices in your life, you'll make the right ones."

"So if I stay here with you, you'd be my dad?" Jacob asked.

Eli nodded. "Though I don't expect you to call me dad, unless that's what you want. Your birth certificate says I'm your father, and I have no intention of changing that. If you really don't want to stay here, then we'll do what we can to work something else out. I'm not sure that going to live with Bobby is an option, however."

Jacob sighed, looking down at his plate. "I kinda hoped I could, but I guess if that was really an option, my mom would have arranged that with Bobby's mom."

"Yes. From the letters your mom left, she made her wishes clear. However, if there is another option that is viable, we'll see what we can do."

"I wanted to go to Bobby's because I didn't think you wanted me here."

"I'm sorry you felt that way." Eli swallowed, hoping to dislodge the lump of emotion in his throat. "We really do want you to stay with us."

"Are you okay staying here now, Jacob?" Kieran asked.

"Yeah. I guess."

It wasn't exactly a ringing endorsement of the plan, but Eli would take it. He knew that Jacob needed time to digest the news he'd overheard, but he had hope that somehow, they'd get through everything. Counseling was definitely in their future, even more necessary now that Jacob had shown he would run away if he got upset or scared.

Eli never wanted Jacob to put himself in danger in order to escape a situation he was worried about. Hopefully, if they could tackle any issues before they got to that point, Jacob would stay safe. Maybe even be happy someday.

"If you're certain, I'm going to head home," Kieran said. "You have my phone number if you need to talk to me."

Jacob nodded. "But I don't have a phone."

"We'll get you one," Eli said. Given that Jacob would be going to school soon, it made sense that he should have a way of contacting them when he was away from the house.

As Kieran got to his feet, Eli did as well and walked with him to the front door.

"Thank you for your help with this," Eli said.

"You're very welcome." Kieran briefly clapped him on the shoulder. "I'll be praying for you all."

"I appreciate that. Here's hoping that we can move forward from this."

"I think you'll be able to. I know you have a good heart, Eli, and will do your best for Jacob and your family."

Eli scrubbed his hands over his face. "I feel like I've already dropped the ball on all of that, but I'll definitely try to do better."

"Call us if you need anything," Kieran said. "You know that we're all here for you."

Eli nodded. He'd been as guilty as Anna of not reaching out for the support that was around them. They were part of a Christian community that he knew would be more than willing to step up should they need the help. Just like he and Anna would offer help to others, should they need it.

His mistake was misjudging how out-of-control everything was. That wouldn't happen again if he could help it.

After Kieran had left, Eli returned to the table, happy to see that Jacob had a cinnamon roll and some fruit on his plate and appeared to be eating it. Eli sank back down in his chair and lifted his mug to take a sip of his coffee.

"I really am sorry I worried you," Jacob murmured as he ripped off a piece of his cinnamon roll. "I wasn't really thinking."

"It's okay. Let's just leave this all in the past and move forward. You're not going to get in trouble for it," Eli reassured him again. "But I hope that if something comes up that makes you want to run away again, you'll talk to someone first. You don't need to come to me or Anna, though we'd like it if you did. You can call Kieran or someone else you trust. I just want you to talk to someone rather than put yourself in danger by running away."

Jacob looked up at him and nodded. They spent the next few minutes eating in silence. Eli still had a knot of worry inside him, but he also had hope. Surely they had nowhere to go but up as they moved forward.

"I guess I was the only one who wasn't smart enough to ask for help," Anna muttered. "Cara has even less help available than me, and yet she knew to take advantage of the help Rose offered her."

"Hey. We're going to declare this house a no-compare zone. You're not allowed to compare yourself to other people, Anna. Especially not other moms." Eli looked at Jacob to find him watching them. "Let's just be who we are and do what works for us. We're a unique family now, and comparisons are just going to be detrimental to us. So, no comparisons, okay?"

He looked at Anna and waited for her to nod, then looked at Jacob. "Okay?"

"Okay."

"Good. We're going to make all of this work. I believe in us."

It took a moment, but then Anna said, "I do too."

"Me, too," Jacob murmured.

Again, not the most confident response, but Eli knew that it was more important that Jacob see that he and Anna believed in their success as a family. It might not be all sunshine and roses. In fact, he was pretty sure it wouldn't be, but even just sporadic moments of sunshine and roses would help to offset the times of struggle.

He felt like God had brought them to this point, so Eli had to believe that He would continue to see them through.

CHAPTER TWENTY

Jacob pressed close to his open locker, using the door to protect himself from the jostling of the groups of students walking by him in the hallway. Though he didn't have homework in all subjects, he didn't want to spend time sorting through his books right then.

His first day at the new school hadn't been too bad. Of course, he'd kept his head down and tried to keep out of the way of everyone. Teachers hadn't made a big deal about him being a new student, for which Jacob was extremely grateful.

The day before, Eli and Anna had taken him shopping for new... well, everything. He'd never had so many clothes that fit so well and were new. Previously, all his clothes had come from thrift stores or had been passed down by Bobby. His mom had always bought his pants and shirts up a size or two, so they'd last longer.

Along with clothes, they'd bought him a bunch of school supplies because whether he liked it or not, he had to go to school. Eli had brought him to register right at the end of the previous school day, and the principal had insisted on showing them around. It had meant that he hadn't stumbled around blindly too much during his first day.

He shoved all of his school stuff into his backpack, then zipped it closed and set it on the floor of the locker so that he could pull on his hoodie. Once he had everything, he spun the lock on the locker, reciting the numbers in his head as he did so.

With a bit of dodging and weaving, he made his way to the front doors of the school. Eli had said he'd be waiting for him instead of making him ride the bus. Jacob didn't know how long that was going to last, but he kinda hoped it would be for a while. Riding the bus without a friend would be a horrible experience if someone decided to pick on him.

Spotting Eli's SUV, Jacob jogged toward it, eager to get back to the house. He opened the door and climbed into the passenger seat, dropping his backpack at his feet.

"How was your first day?" Eli asked as he slowly maneuvered the SUV away from the curb.

"It was alright."

Eli glanced at him. "Make a friend?"

"No, but I didn't really expect to."

"Why's that?"

Jacob shrugged. "I just figure it will probably take some time to find someone who's nice and likes the same stuff I do."

"I'm sure that there's at least one person who meets those requirements."

"I hope so."

As they drove back to the house, Eli shared about his experiences in the schools of New Hope Falls. Because it was a smaller town, he'd known most of the kids in each year of school.

Even though it hadn't been a bad day, Jacob still wished that Bobby had been there with him. Recess and lunch had been the worst parts of the day because he'd had to spend them by himself. Thankfully, he'd had his new phone to keep him company. No one had to know that he was playing a game of matching candies instead of doing something cool, like talking to a friend.

When they got home, Anna greeted him with a smile and a plate of cookies that she said Nadine had dropped off in celebration of his first day at school. After running his backpack up to his room, he returned to the living room, where his cookies and hot chocolate waited.

He sat down on the floor next to Noah, who was in his bouncy seat. "Hey, buddy. Did you have a good day?"

Noah squealed in response, bouncing and waving his arms around.

"He's been living it up as usual," Anna said with a laugh. "How was your day, Jacob?"

"Could've been worse," he told her as he picked up a cookie and broke off a piece. "No one beat me up."

"I'm very glad to hear that." Anna moved to sit on the floor across the coffee table from him. She took a cookie from the plate. "What are your classes like? Do your teachers seem nice?"

Jacob thought back over the classes he'd had that day. "Most seem okay. The math teacher seems a little weird, though."

"Weird, how?"

"He wears a bow tie and suspenders with his jeans."

"Is he an older man?"

"Not really. Older than you guys, but not like grandpa old."

Anna chuckled as she took a bite of cookie. "Sounds like an interesting person."

"One can only hope, since I can't stand math."

"What subjects *do* you like?"

"I like science. Doing the experiments, anyway."

"My cooking has felt like experiments at times."

"Uh... maybe that's not something you should admit? Especially to someone who has to eat it?"

Anna laughed again. "Yeah. Probably not. I'm just so tired most days that I think I forget ingredients."

"I could start doing some cooking," Jacob said, a bit surprised at how much the idea appealed to him. It was different to think about cooking when he could use actual ingredients and would be doing it because he wanted to. Cooking mac and cheese or ramen because he had to if he wanted to eat hadn't been much fun.

"Don't be making me offers like that unless you plan to follow through," Anna warned, her words ending with a yawn.

"Maybe... uh... Nadine would help me learn more."

Anna rested her arms on the coffee table. "If you really want to learn how to cook, Nadine's the best one to teach you."

"I don't want to get in anyone's way."

"Right now, it's not too busy at the lodge. At least during the week. I think we'll probably be eating at the lodge more, now that I'm willing to admit that I'm... struggling. Even though I feel like I should be the one cooking meals for us."

"Do you love Noah?"

Anna frowned at him. "Of course."

"And you're trying to do the best for him?"

"Well, yes."

"Then it's not going to matter that you're not cooking meals for him. For us. My mom wasn't able to buy me great stuff or do a lot for me, but I always knew she was doing her best, even when she was struggling. That she loved me."

"You miss her a lot."

Jacob was glad she didn't phrase it as a question. As if, because of how his mom had died, he might not miss her. "Yeah. I do."

"Tell me about her."

"Really?" Jacob had a hard time believing that Anna would want to hear about the woman who had messed up her life by making her husband take on a son who wasn't really his.

"Yes. Really."

Jacob looked down at his cup of hot chocolate, pulling up the happy memories he had of his mom. "She liked being in the sun. She used to tell me that growing up, she lived somewhere that had a lot of cloudy, drizzly days. I see now what she meant."

"This *can* be a rather wet place to live. It's made me cherish the moments of sunshine we get."

"Yeah. She said that too. Rainy days were... bad for her. Sometimes she wouldn't even get out of bed. The weather seemed to affect her mood more than it did for most people."

176 · KIMBERLY RAE JORDAN

He'd hated those days the most because there was literally nothing he could do to help her. It wasn't like he could magically change the weather.

He didn't say anything more. *Couldn't* say anything more as he remembered that feeling of helplessness.

"I know it's probably not easy to think of her right now," Anna said, her voice soft. "But hopefully, in time, you'll be able to focus on the happier moments you had with her."

He nodded, not bothering to tell her that most of the happy memories he had with his mom were when he was younger. In recent years, her slide into depression had only gotten worse, so their fun and happy moments had become fewer. In the past year, they'd been pretty much non-existent.

"Do you have homework?" Anna asked when he didn't volunteer any further information about his mom.

"A little bit."

"Did you want to talk to Bobby?"

"Can I?"

"We'll have to leave for the lodge in about half an hour, so if you want to talk to him before we go, you can. Then when we come home, you can do your homework."

He nodded his understanding, then picked up his empty mug and got to his feet. He rinsed the mug out and put it in the dishwasher. Before going upstairs, he grabbed another cookie, then bent down to ruffle Noah's hair. Noah squealed in response, making Jacob smile.

Upstairs in his room, Jacob dropped down on his bed and pulled his phone out of his backpack. Bobby didn't have his own phone, but he did have a tablet that had a video chat program that they used. He'd talked to him the day the police chief had brought him home, and he'd been so relieved that Jacob was alright.

"Hey!" Bobby said as his face filled the screen. "How's it going? Was school okay?"

Jacob shrugged. "About as good as I expected. Nobody talked to me, but nobody teased me either, so I'm calling it a win."

"Definitely." They talked a bit more about their day, then Jacob had to go. "I'll talk to you maybe tomorrow."

Bobby gave him a thumbs up, then they ended their call. Jacob went back downstairs, making it in the half hour timeframe that Anna had given him.

At the lodge, Jacob immediately offered his help, and Nadine didn't hesitate to put him to work setting the table. He would have preferred to help with the cooking, but since they hadn't arrived early enough, the meal was already prepared.

"Mom, I just got off a call," Leah said as she walked by Jacob, offering him a quick hug. "The name sounded familiar, but I can't place it. They want to rent everything for a family gathering."

"What's the name?" Nadine asked as she gave Jacob a basket that held the cutlery.

"The woman said she was Cathy Halverson."

Jacob didn't miss the grimace that crossed Nadine's face, and apparently neither did Leah.

"Who is she?"

Nadine sighed, her shoulders slumping in a way that Jacob didn't like. The older woman had only ever shown happiness around him, and he found that her unhappiness didn't sit well with him.

"Cathy used to live in New Hope, and she was one of my best friends. She left for college, where she met the man she ended up marrying."

"Wait," Eli said, holding his hand up. "Didn't we go visit them when I was in high school?"

Nadine nodded. "We'd visited back and forth a bit, but then life kind of took over. She and her husband were busy with their practice—they're both doctors—and they had a large family, so travel wasn't always easy. That trip you're talking about, Eli, was our last trip to see them. When your dad left, I just didn't feel like leaving the lodge anymore."

"I wonder why they're coming here?" Eli asked. "Did they just say a family gathering, Leah?"

"Yep. She just wanted to know if we had a time where everything was available. The lodge and the cabins, since there would be twelve or so people coming."

"They do still have some family in the area," Nadine said. "So they could be coming for a reunion or something. I haven't talked to any of Cathy's family lately, though, so I don't know."

"Well, I told her that the stretch of January through March was our least busy time," Leah said. "But if you'd prefer them not to come, Mom, I'll let her know that it won't work."

"It's not that I don't want to see her—them—again," Nadine said. "It's just that it was hard to be around them after everything that happened with your dad and then with Eli. I kind of let contact lapse over the years."

"You ghosted her?" Leah asked.

Nadine frowned. "Ghosted? What's that?"

"It's when you kind of just stop communicating with someone without explanation."

"Well, I guess that's what I did then." Nadine sighed. "Not very mature of me, I know, but I just kind of withdrew from a lot of people who weren't family during that time."

Eli nodded, then went to wrap his arms around his mom. "Well, whatever you decide about this family coming to the lodge, we'll support you."

Nadine hugged Eli back, seeming to lean on him for a moment before stepping back. "Thanks, sweetie. I think maybe it's time to reconnect with Cathy. I'm in a better place now."

Jacob headed into the dining room with his basket of cutlery and began to set the table. As he did that, he considered what it must be like to have a place like the lodge. It was clear that every-one had a role.

Now that he knew that Eli and Anna wanted him to be part of their family, he hoped that maybe he could have a part in what they did at the lodge, too. The idea of being part of the work they did there appealed to him a lot.

When he went back into the kitchen after finishing the table, Nadine gave him a tight squeeze before grasping his shoulders and smiling at him. "Thank you for doing that. I appreciate your help."

"You're welcome. Can I do something else?"

"Not just yet."

Jacob moved to sit on one of the stools, so he was out of the way, but close enough if Nadine had another task for him. Anna approached him with Noah on her hip.

Noah reached for Jacob, but he wasn't sure if he should take him, so he just played with his hands. Anna, however, leaned forward with Noah. "Do you think you can handle him?"

"I'm not sure."

"Go ahead and take him," she said. "I'll stay close in case he gets out of control."

Jacob couldn't believe she was trusting him with Noah, but he supposed that if he and Noah were to be brothers, he'd have to learn how to take care of him.

Brothers. He'd always felt like Bobby was a brother, which was why he missed him so much. With Noah being a baby, he would never replace Bobby, but Jacob liked the idea of having a younger brother.

Anna helped him situate Noah on his lap, facing the counter. Jacob kept his arms around him, fingers interlocked over his chubby belly. After all the emotional upheaval of the past few weeks, he finally had a feeling of peace. It didn't erase his grief, and in some ways, that peace made him feel the grief even more. But he knew now that these people would allow him to grieve, and that they would support him through the ups and downs of this new life without his mom.

~*~

Eli poured coffee into the mug sitting on the counter, then took Noah from Anna and handed her the mug. She thanked him before going to the table and slumping down into one of the chairs.

It had been another rough night, and they had a busy day ahead. They had to drop Noah off with Nadine, then take Jacob to school. After that, Anna had a doctor's appointment, followed by a session with her therapist. He'd go with her to the doctor's appointment, but not to the therapist.

For now, she needed to speak with the therapist on her own. Maybe there would come a time when she wanted Eli with her, and if that day came, he'd happily agree. Anything to help get Anna back to a spot where she felt like herself again. Soon they'd be adding trips to the therapist for Jacob, since he'd agreed to see the person Ryker had recommended.

With Noah propped on his hip, Eli prepared a bottle for him, then took him to his highchair next to Anna. Once he was settled with his bottle, Eli went back to get some breakfast ready for Jacob before they left.

Jacob showed up a few minutes later, and with Eli's help, he put together a lunch. They did have a cafeteria at the school, but Jacob seemed to prefer bringing something from home.

He handed Jacob a plate with an egg, toast, and some sausages, then carried plates for Anna and himself to the table. After he said a blessing for the food, they ate in silence. Jacob wasn't super chatty, which Eli related to. He had never been very talkative as a teen, either.

Once they were done eating, Eli took Noah to change him while Anna got ready. Jacob seemed to have no problem loading the dishes into the dishwasher while Eli and Anna were busy.

By the time they were ready to leave, Jacob had cleared up everything from breakfast. They piled into the SUV, then headed toward the lodge to drop Noah off. Eli took him in while Anna and Jacob waited in the car.

On the drive to Jacob's school, Anna said, "Are you ready for your second day of school?"

"I suppose. I got my homework done, and I think I remembered everything."

"I hope that you're able to connect with a friend or two."

"Maybe. I just want to make it through the day without anyone bugging me."

"I think we're all just trying to get through this day," she said, then laid her hand on Eli's arm. "Are we going to the lodge for dinner?"

"Yep. Mom said we should just plan to be there each night. I think she enjoys the company, plus Leah and Gavin will be there most nights, too."

"Make sure you give her some money to help with groceries," Anna said. "It's not really fair that she foots the bill for us eating there."

"I tell you what," Eli said with a laugh. "You can be the one to offer that to her."

"I just don't want to take advantage of her."

"You're not taking advantage if she's offering it. She wants us there. She wants to have Noah and Jacob around. So don't worry about that. I think it's been weird for her to not have any family in the lodge after Leah and Gavin got married. The empty nest is really getting to her."

"She'll tell us if it's too much, right?"

Eli nodded. "I told her that the only way I felt comfortable taking advantage of her offer to help was if she let us know when she couldn't. She agreed to be honest about that."

"I hope that's what happens."

When Eli pulled up in front of the school, he glanced into the rear-view mirror to see Jacob staring out the window at the kids walking toward the building. Most were in groups, but Jacob would walk in alone.

He exchanged a glance with Anna, but neither of them said anything until Jacob opened the door. "Have a good day, Jacob."

"I'll try." He looked over his shoulder at them as he climbed out. "See you later."

Eli watched as Jacob walked up the sidewalk, his head down and his shoulders hunched. His heart hurt for the teen, knowing that even though he wasn't saying it, attending the new school was stressful for him.

Anna reached out and threaded her fingers with his. "Let's pray for him."

Eli nodded, waiting until Jacob disappeared through the front door of the school, then bowing his head and praying.

"Heavenly Father, we ask you to make Your presence known to Jacob today and ease the anxiety that he's probably feeling. We pray that there might be someone who is interested in befriending him. Also, protect him from anyone who might want to hurt or tease him. We look forward to seeing how You work in Jacob's life. In Jesus' name, amen."

Anna sighed. "I really feel for him."

"I do too, but he needs to be in school."

"I know. Hopefully, he has something positive to share when we pick him up later."

Eli guided the SUV around the curb. Despite busy days, life felt like it was calming down. However, having Jacob settled at school would go a long way toward Eli feeling like things really were going to work out. He was confident that Jacob wouldn't run away again, but he wanted the boy to be happy in his life, too. As happy as a grieving teen could be, anyway.

As he considered the future, Eli knew it wouldn't be without its ups and downs. However, he was confident that the love he shared with Anna would continue to be a good foundation for whatever came. God had proven His faithfulness to them through the people around them, providing them with the support they needed. And he believed that the love they now shared with Jacob would help him find a place in the new life he'd been thrust into because of his mother's death.

EPILOGUE

Late February

Jacob opened the door of the SUV, glancing back at his dad as he slid to the ground. "I'll see you in a bit."

"Yep. I'll be back once I pick up Anna and Noah."

He nodded, then moved his backpack up onto his shoulder before shutting the door. There weren't any unfamiliar vehicles in front of the lodge, but that would change soon. They were expecting a large influx of people in the next couple of hours. That was one of the reasons he was there. To help Nadine prepare dinner for the guests.

Inside the lodge, the aromatic warmth wrapped around him, making him smile and chasing away the chill of the rainy, dreary day. The sense of being home was as strong at the lodge as it was in Eli and Anna's house.

"Hello, my darling," Nadine said as she greeted him with a smile and a tight hug. He might not have been her blood grandchild, but she never treated him any differently than she did Noah. "How was your day?"

"It was fine." Jacob put his backpack in the corner under the counter, then went to the sink to wash his hands. "I think I did okay on my science test, but not sure about my math quiz."

"Still not liking the subject?" Nadine asked.

Jacob took the towel she held out and dried his hands. "Nope. The teacher isn't so bad—outside of his sense of style—but I just don't understand what he teaches most of the time."

"You should ask Beau for help again," Nadine said. "He really loves his numbers."

Beau had helped him out a while back, but Jacob knew he was busy with his business and didn't like to bug him for help. It made him feel so stupid that he couldn't grasp a lot of what the teacher taught. Thankfully, Eli and Anna seemed to understand his struggle with the subject and offered what help they could.

"Maybe," Jacob murmured.

"Ready to do something not completely math oriented?" Nadine asked.

"Most definitely."

"Great! We're having baked chicken with mashed potatoes and roasted veggies for dinner."

For the next little while, Jacob followed Nadine's instructions as they worked together to fill large pans with pieces of chicken dipped in eggs and breadcrumbs seasoned with an assortment of spices. Once that was done, he helped her cut up the potatoes that she'd peeled before he got there.

"What's for dessert?" he asked.

"Leah made a crumble with all the apples we got at the store earlier this week."

Jacob loved Leah's desserts, and what he loved even more was when she let him help her. Since he had started to help with cooking at the lodge, he'd also started to eat more.

Anna had joked that she was having to buy him bigger clothes at the same rate she was having to buy them for Noah. Still, she'd insisted on getting him brand name clothes that he'd never had before, even knowing that he might grow out of them quickly.

Hearing the front door open, followed by unfamiliar voices, Jacob glanced at Nadine, knowing that these were the guests she'd been apprehensive about having when they'd first called a few months earlier. Nadine set her knife down and moved toward the sink to wash her hands. Before she could even dry them, a man and woman Nadine's age walked into the kitchen.

"Nadine!" The woman's face lit with a smile, and with open arms, she approached Nadine.

Jacob watched the women hug as more people of varying ages and ethnicities came to stand in the doorway to the kitchen. Tightly gripping the knife he held, Jacob turned his attention back to the potato he was cutting.

"I'm so happy to see you again," the other woman said. "Thank you for putting us all up in your beautiful lodge."

"You're more than welcome here, Cathy. I'm glad you could make it."

The man stepped forward, holding his hand out. "Good to see you again, Nadine."

"You too, Dan." Nadine shook his hand. "How have you been?"

"I've been good. You?"

"Doing really well."

"Do you remember our kids?" Cathy asked, waving a hand to the group standing behind her.

"I'm not sure I'd pass a quiz on names," Nadine admitted with a laugh.

"There are days I don't think I would either. I run through all their names just to get to the one I need." Cathy's face seemed given to smiles. "As I say your name, raise your hand so Nadine knows for sure who I'm talking about."

Jacob paused again, listening as Cathy rattled off names, matching them to the person who raised their hand. A couple of them looked like maybe they were just two or three years older than him. Others looked to be around Eli, Leah, and Sarah's age. It seemed they had kids who were adopted because there was definitely a mix of races.

"My kids should be here soon, but I do have one of my two grandsons here helping me out," Nadine said as she moved to stand next to him, laying her arm across his shoulder. "This is Jacob. He is Eli's oldest."

Cathy smiled at him. "Nice to meet you, Jacob."

"You too," Jacob said with a nod of his head. He was a bit overwhelmed by so many people, but Nadine's claiming of him as her grandson helped to calm his nervousness.

"Will you be okay finishing up the potatoes?" Nadine asked.

Jacob nodded. "I'll get them done."

"Thanks, darling." She pressed a kiss to his head. "I'll be back soon."

As she led the guests from the room, Jacob got back to work on the potatoes, determined to have them all finished by the time Nadine got back. She was relying on him, and Jacob didn't want to let her down.

He'd never thought much about having a grandma. Bobby hadn't had grandparents he spent time with, so Jacob hadn't known what having a grandparent would be like. Of course, his actual grandparents had nothing to do with him, even though they didn't live very far away.

Josie had explained that whole situation to him, and while it would have been nice to have more grandparents, Jacob wasn't too excited about having to deal with someone who had worse mental issues than his mom had dealt with. That thought might make him selfish, but his therapist had said that it was okay for him to want to keep his distance from them. Considering that his grandfather had yet to meet him, Jacob figured if they could want to keep their distance from him, then he could do that as well.

The front door opened again, but this time, it was familiar faces who appeared.

"Hey, Jake," Anna said as she came in with his dad behind her carrying Noah.

He set his knife down and dried his hands before giving Anna a hug. His dad set Noah down on the floor, and the baby crawled right over to where Jacob stood. Noah grabbed onto Jacob's jeans and pulled himself up to stand on his wobbly legs. Jacob lifted him up with ease and settled him on his hip.

Noah clapped his hands on Jacob's cheeks, a big smile on his face. Bobby couldn't understand how Jacob could care about a baby who couldn't really do anything with him. And honestly, Jacob couldn't explain it either. All he knew was that he loved Noah, and even though they weren't blood brothers, he would always consider Noah as such.

"Hey, buddy. What have you been drooling all over today?"

"Me," Anna said. "He's been drooling all over me today. Teething never gets more fun."

Jacob grinned, then handed Noah to Anna. "Well, I don't think anyone wants drool on their potatoes, so you better hang with Mama."

"I see our guests have arrived," his dad said.

"Yep. Grandma is showing them around."

"Can we do anything to help you?" Anna asked.

The idea that she thought he had some sort of say in what needed to be done made him smile. Unfortunately, he had no clue. "I'm not sure."

Thankfully, Leah arrived with Gavin, and she stepped right in, instructing him to fill the pots of potatoes with water and set them on the stove. Anna handed Noah off to his dad, then moved to the sink to help Jacob while Leah slid the pans of chicken into the oven.

"Sarah's not here yet?" Leah asked. "Or is she helping Mom?"

"I haven't seen her," Jacob said. "It was just Grandma here when I arrived."

Leah gave him a quick hug. "How're you doing?"

"I'm good."

"Glad to hear it."

Leah and Sarah had accepted him, just like their mom had, and it made him feel even more like he had a place in their world. He'd also found a couple of friends at school and church. He wasn't as close to them as he was to Bobby, but he had fun hanging out with them.

The only downside to his life currently—aside from the loss of his mom—was that he hadn't been able to see Bobby, and since their schools' spring breaks didn't line up, it would probably be summer before they got to hang out together again. Still, he talked to him nearly every day, and they played video games together all the time. Sometimes, they even played with his new friends.

Grief was still a large part of his life, but it came and went. Sometimes the steady dull ache pulsed more painfully. They hadn't buried her ashes yet. After talking with Eli and Anna, he'd decided to wait until it was warmer to do it. Hopefully on a bright, sunny day, since his mom had always loved those kinds of days.

He struggled at times to not wish things had turned out differently for him and his mom. But his therapist had told him that thinking like that would just confuse and upset him when wishing for things to be different couldn't change anything anyways. Everything that had happened—good and bad—could never be changed, and he had to accept that in order to embrace his new life and move forward.

Some days, that was easier to do than others. On days like that one, where his place in the McNamara world seemed solid, it was easier to accept everything that had happened. He hoped that his mom would be happy with how things had turned out for him, since she was the one who had set all of it in motion.

~*~

Anna curled into Eli's side, her gaze on the flickering flames in the fireplace in front of them. Contentment helped ease the tiredness as she relished the feel of his strong arm curved around her, the familiar scent of his body wash surrounding her.

"How was your day?" Eli asked after he pressed a kiss to the top of her head.

"Well, I wasn't sure how it was going to go when I woke up later than I planned, but then this handsome man made me a delicious breakfast, and everything was better."

Eli chuckled softly. "I'm glad you enjoyed it."

"Unfortunately, Noah is on a nap strike again, which made him incredibly cranky today."

"This too shall pass, right?" Eli said. "You'll get some sleep to-night, since it's my turn to be on nursery duty."

Anna hated the idea of not having Eli in the bed with her, but they'd had to work out a plan that helped them deal with Noah's fractured nights. Rather than both of them having their sleep inter-rupted each night, they'd decided to take turns staying in Noah's room, sleeping on the twin bed they'd purchased and set up in the nursery.

He'd actually gotten better at sleeping over the past couple of months, so the bed hadn't gotten a lot of use. But every time he began to teeth, his sleep was the first thing to suffer. She prayed that this latest bout of teething passed quickly, so they didn't have to do the night sharing for too much longer.

"How was Jacob's day?" Anna asked. "I didn't get a chance to talk much to him today."

"School was okay, he said. I think he got a better grade on his math test than he thought he would after bombing his quiz last week. Beau's help must have made the difference."

"Nadine mentioned that he has been a huge help to her this week, too, with all the people at the lodge."

"I'm so proud of him for how willing he's been to pitch in and help. Mom said she's really come to depend on him."

Anna smiled. Jacob seemed to really enjoy helping at the lodge. In particular, he enjoyed cooking or baking, but he also pitched in to help wherever he was needed. It was good because Anna still wasn't back to being able to help Nadine as much as she had before getting pregnant.

"He has therapy tomorrow, right?" Anna said.

"Yeah. He asked if he could change his appointment from Wednesday so that he could help Mom. But all the Halversons left today, so he has more free time to see the therapist tomorrow."

Jacob's therapy had seemed to help the teen. He rarely talked about what he and his therapist discussed, but Anna could see positive changes in him. Just like her therapy was helping her.

The three of them had gone to a handful of sessions together, but they didn't seem to need to go as a family regularly, so the solo appointments for Anna and Jacob were more the norm. Jacob knew that he was welcome to request a family session at any time if there was something specific he wanted to discuss with them and felt it would be better with his therapist present.

"How are you doing, love?" Anna asked, resting her hand on his chest. "Did you get that order sorted out at the gallery?"

Eli covered her hand with his, giving her fingers a light squeeze. "Yep. Took a while for them to be able to voice what they wanted, but we got there."

This time of each day had become her favorite. Along with the other changes in her life, setting aside time with Eli each day had played a significant role in her getting a handle on her postpartum depression. It helped her to remember that no matter how bad her day might have been, Eli was there for her.

It was something the therapist had suggested early in their sessions, and Eli had been completely on board with the idea. He made sure that Noah was asleep, and Jacob was occupied with homework or Bobby. He'd explained to Jacob about it being 'couple time' for just the two of them, and the teen had been re-spectful of it.

Something she'd learned about herself through the past several months was that, for all that she'd felt like she had to stand on her own, she really needed a connection to keep a balance in her life. For her, that was both her connection to God and to Eli. Sharing with each other how they were feeling had become an essential part of their day.

They also took the time to discuss what was going on in their respective careers. Eli's woodworking business was steady, and he managed to fit his work in around the work he did at the lodge. Anna was back to doing regular videos and other posts on social media. It had taken awhile to figure out how to balance her new reality with what people wanted to see from her on her YouTube channel, and sometimes she still struggled. But she pushed through as best she could.

Jacob had been surprised to learn that she was a "YouTuber" with a significant following on the platform. Surprised and im-pressed. She'd ended up doing a video devoted to male teen fashion, using him as her model. That had been a fun project for the two of them, and it had helped them bond, bringing a new closeness to their relationship.

"Other than being tired, are you doing okay?" Eli asked.

"Yeah. I cried today, though." Eli's arm tightened around her. "It's just so hard when Noah is inconsolable. Nothing worked to settle him. Not a bath. Not his bottle. Not holding him. It was just... hard. So when he was crying, I cried too."

"I'm sorry I wasn't here to help more," Eli said.

Anna shook her head. "It's fine. I eventually put him in the stroller and took him for a walk with Shadow. I think the fresh air did us good. We both settled for a little while. Didn't last forever, of course, but I was grateful for the reprieve."

"You are such a good mom," Eli said, pulling her more closely against him. "I know you don't feel that way sometimes, but you are."

Anna shifted to face him more fully and smiled up at him. "You're right. I don't always feel that way, but I know that I couldn't do this without you. And when I see you with Noah and Jacob, I thank God that you are the father of our children. They are so blessed to have you. Just like I am."

She leaned forward and pressed her lips to his. It had come as a surprise that parenting with Eli could draw them even closer together. That hadn't been the case at first, of course. But once they'd gotten back on track, their love had deepened even more, providing a stable foundation for them to love and raise the two boys that God had given to them.

She'd also discovered over the past several months that love wasn't a finite thing. She hadn't been sure if she'd be able to love a child who wasn't hers the way she loved Noah. Thankfully, nothing could have been further from the truth. Jacob was as much her son as Noah was, and even though he didn't call her Mom, he would always be her son.

Once she and Eli had opened their hearts more fully to each other, the love they had for Noah and Jacob had flowed so easily. And even though they had rough parenting moments at times, she knew that their family wasn't complete. She wasn't sure how God would grow their family, but she knew that they all had more love to share.

"I love you," Eli whispered against her lips, then pulled back, cupping her face in his hands. His gaze was filled with love, and warmth spiraled through Anna. "I never imagined I'd have so much love in my life."

As they continued to cuddle on the couch, Anna let the love she felt for Eli flow through their physical connection. Never had she felt more secure in their love and in God's guidance in their lives.

She was sad that it had taken such a horrible loss for Jacob in order to bring their family together, but she was grateful that Sheila had made sure that Jacob came to Eli.

Grief still had a place in their lives because they wanted Jacob to feel free to express his feelings with regards to the loss of his mom. Walking through that grief with him had given them experiences that Anna was certain would stand them in good stead in the years to come.

Love was their foundation. God's love for them. Their love for each other. Their love for their family. She wanted to always remember that love grew the more it was shared, and love could be the oil that kept relationships running smoothly. And more than anything, Anna wanted their family to flourish, offering a safe and happy place for both their boys—and any other children God gave them—to grow up in.

ABOUT THE AUTHOR

Kimberly Rae Jordan is a USA Today bestselling author of Christian romances. Many years ago, her love of reading Christian romance morphed into a desire to write stories of love, faith, and family, and thus began a journey that would lead her to places Kimberly never imagined she'd go.

In addition to being a writer, she is also a wife and mother, which means Kimberly spends her days straddling the line between real life in a house on the prairies of Canada and the imaginary world her characters live in. Though caring for her husband and four kids and working on her stories takes up a large portion of her day, Kimberly also enjoys reading and looking at craft ideas that she will likely never attempt to make.

As she continues to pen heartwarming stories of love, faith, and family, Kimberly hopes that readers of all ages will enjoy the journeys her characters take in each book. She has no plan to stop writing the stories God places on her heart and looks forward to where her journey will take her in the years to come.

www.ingramcontent.com/pod-product-compliance
Lightning Source LLC
Chambersburg PA
CBHW021958190626
46808CB00017B/2243